The ONLY GIRL in school

natalie
standiford

The ONLY GIRL in school

illustrations by nathan durfee

Scholastic Inc.

Text copyright © 2016 by Natalie Standiford
Illustrations copyright © 2016 by Nathan Durfee

This book was originally published in hardcover by Scholastic Press in 2016.

All rights reserved. Published by Scholastic Inc., *Publishers since 1920.* SCHOLASTIC and associated logos are trademarks and/or registered trademarks of Scholastic Inc.

The publisher does not have any control over and does not assume any responsibility for author or third-party websites or their content.

ISBN 978-0-545-82997-7

10 9 8 7 6 5 4 3 2 1   18 19 20 21 22

Printed in the U.S.A.   40
First printing 2018

Book design by Nina Goffi

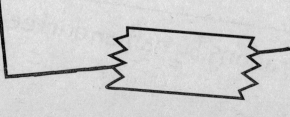

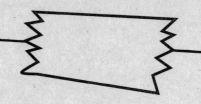

For my only niece, Natalie Jane.
And for my father, who loves
the Chesapeake Bay.

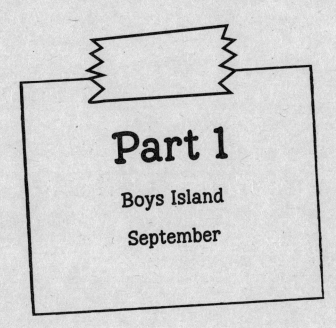

Part 1

Boys Island

September

Yucky Gilbert Sits Next to Me

To: *Bess Calhoun*
San Francisco, California

From: *Claire Warren*
Foyes Island, Maryland

Dear Bess,

Here's how I imagine your first day of school:

You hated it. The kids are mean. Your teacher is mean. And boring. It's very strict with lots of dumb rules that make no sense, like *No one is allowed to go to the bathroom without a buddy.* Which means you can never go to the bathroom at school, ever, because there is no other girl IN THE WHOLE ENTIRE SCHOOL to be your bathroom buddy.

Oh, wait. That was MY first day.

But you hated yours too, right? Please say you are begging your parents to move back to Foyes Island right now. If they don't move back, you'll run away and live here with me.

I miss you. Can you tell?

I know it's not your fault you moved away. And I know it's not your fault that our town is so small and our school is so teeny and that through some freak coincidence, all the other students happen to be boys. It wasn't bad when it was just the two of us. I liked it when it was the two of us.

I do not like it when it's just the one of me.

I thought it might be SORT OF okay because I still had Henry. You know, Henry Long, the third-fastest sailor on Foyes Island (after me and you), my other best friend? Ha ha ha.

Henry was supposed to pick me up this morning so we could walk to school together, just like we've done every school day since first grade. Only this year Gabe was going to go with us. Gaby was wearing a bow tie and everything, in honor of his first day of first grade. He's a cute little dork.

Gabe and I waited on our front porch for an hour.

No Henry.

Finally it was 8:15 and Henry still hadn't showed. Poor Gaby was frantic. He didn't want to start his very first day of school ever, not counting kindergarten, by being late. He kept saying, "My teacher will think I'm bad and I'll never be able to change her mind!"

"Don't worry," I told him. "He'll be here soon. Henry never lets me down."

Mom came out and said, "You're still here? You're going to be late for your first day!" So Gabe and I gave up on Henry and ran all the way to school. The whole time I was thinking, *What happened to Henry? Oh my gosh I hope he's okay!!!!! What if he got hit by a car on the way to my house? What if he's got a deadly bacterial infection? What if he died???!!!?*

Because what else could keep Henry from walking to school with me, just like always? What else besides the end of the world?

But when I got to school, there he was, hanging out by his locker with Webby and those guys, perfectly safe and healthy and not the least bit dead.

"Henry!" I was shocked. I couldn't understand what he was doing there.

"Oh, hi, Claire." He said it all casual, like, *Oh, hi, Person I Barely Know.*

It doesn't make any sense, does it?

I stood in the hall for what felt like a million seconds, flapping my jaw open and closed, trying to understand why Henry was acting so weird. Finally I said, "Henry, what are you doing here?"

"What do you mean?" he asked, like it was the stupidest question he'd ever heard. "It's, you know, school."

"Yeah, so why didn't you stop at my house to walk over with me like you always do?"

As soon as I asked this, Webby snort-laughed. I officially hate Webby and his snort-laugh. Since when is Henry friends with him anyway?

"I don't know what you're talking about," Henry told me.

Before I could ask him if he'd had a brain transplant over the summer, or at least a complete memory wipe, the bell rang. We had to go to class. Webby and Henry walked into Mr. Harper's room and sat down next to each other. Henry took an end seat, so I couldn't sit on his other side.

I sat down in the second row. The seat next to me was the last free desk in the room. It was strange to see boys all around me, and to be the only girl. When you were here, it wasn't as obvious, because I could compare what I was wearing to what you were wearing, or I could flash a look your way, and you'd know what I meant. I was not the only creature of my kind. But now I'm like an alien, a castaway from the planet Girl, stranded on Boys Island.

I counted the number of kids in the class: six boys and me. There was one boy missing. I looked around to see where Yucky Gilbert was . . . and he wasn't in class yet.

Oh no.

Oh yes.

Mr. Harper was just closing the door when Yucky Gilbert ran in. Yucky G. looked around for an empty seat, spotted the one next to me, and grinned so wide the sunlight flashed off his braces, temporarily blinding me. He dashed over to plant his butt next to mine. He smacked his slobbery lips and said, "Hi, Claire." There was a little string of drool dripping off his braces, between his upper teeth and his lower teeth. It stretched while he talked but never broke. Yucky Gilbert's drool is strong, like a spider's web.

6

I read his mind. Here's what he was thinking:

Hi, Claire. Welcome to another year of me constantly trying to kiss you. And this year I'm going to triumph.

I swear, Bessie, I could see it in his eyes.

What am I going to do? I used to have you and Henry to shield me from Yucky G., but now you're three thousand miles away and Henry is acting like I don't exist. I pray that Mr. Harper won't make us keep these seats permanently for the rest of the year. Because if I have to spend a whole year fending off Yucky G., my life will be one continuous saliva shower.

I know you're squirming and gagging and saying, "Claire stop being gross," so I'll stop the Yucky G. Report for today.

Later tater,
Claire

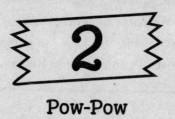

2

Pow-Pow

Day One, continued

Dear Bess,

I know this letter is really long, but a lot happened today and almost ALL of it was HORRIBLE.

While Mr. Harper was telling us about the upcoming school year, I could hear Y.G. slobbering over his braces and feel him staring at me with his big, googly blue eyes. Then it was time for gym.

Mr. Harper shouted at us to file out in an orderly fashion, but we didn't. We burst screaming into the hallway. I turned around and Gilbert was RIGHT behind me, practically glued to my back. His lips are always wet. His freckles look like tiny fleas on his face. We should call him Flea Face. He grinned, and then puckered up and leaned forward. He was trying to kiss me right there in the hallway!

Mr. Unitas was walking by just at that moment. I thought, *Oh good, the principal*. He'll *save me.*

I cried, "Mr. Unitas, help!"

8

But Mr. Unitas hardly even looked down at us. He just patted me and Gilbert on the back.

"Good to see you again, kids," he told us. "Let's have a productive year this year!"

He swam through the flood of kids mobbing the hallway, his eyes straight ahead, not looking any of us in the face. I guess you can get away with that when you're really tall and built like a football player.

At least it stopped Yucky G. from getting close enough to make contact. I was happy for about three seconds.

Then I got to gym.

You know how I feel about gym. Gym is never good.

Today, Mr. Powell was in a great mood. Which is like saying a shark is in a great mood. Or a tiger. Their mood is not really the point.

"Let's take it easy and have some fun, huh, kids?" Pow-Pow offered. "How about a little game of dodgeball?"

I used to like dodgeball. Those days are over.

Anyway, this game wasn't really dodgeball. It was more like Pummel the Girl.

Team captain: Webby Peterson.

Pow-Pow divided us into two teams and put three balls on the centerline of the basketball court. I was on Webby's team. So was Henry. Gilbert was on the other team.

Webby and Zach M. raced to the line and snatched up two balls. Cal grabbed a ball for the other team. We all ran back to our sides of the court. Cal threw his ball at me, but it bounced and I caught it. I was winding up to throw the ball at Gilbert when a ball bonked me on the back. I turned around. Webby was grinning at me. "You're out."

"But I'm on your team!" I protested.

Webby didn't care. "Rules are rules," he said. "Henry, throw your ball at her."

"No, Henry!" I countered. I was sure he could see how unfair this was. You're not supposed to throw the ball at your own teammates! I looked at Mr. Powell but he was just standing on the sidelines with his fist on his hip, staring at his phone.

Henry threw his ball at me, hard. That made me mad. I threw my ball at him.

"Mr. Powell!" Webby shouted. "Claire is throwing the ball at us!"

Tattletale!

Pow-Pow didn't even look up. Which Webby took as permission to scream, "Get her!"

All the boys—my team, the other team—threw balls at me. One ball would bounce off me and another boy would catch it and throw it back at me. I shielded my face and shouted, *"This isn't how you play dodgeball!* Mr. Powell! Mr. Powell!"

FINALLY Mr. Powell blew his whistle. I thought, *Okay, good, justice,* but then he hollered, "Claire Warren, you're out!"

"But, Mr. Pow—"

"Go on." He ushered me toward the bleachers. I

didn't protest. At least if I was out I would be safe from getting pummeled.

Or at least that's what I thought.

Pow-Pow blew his whistle again. "Resume play!"

Then he resumed his texting. Or whatever he was doing on his phone.

The boys picked up the balls and bounced them on the floor. Yucky Gilbert had one, but Webby took it from him. The other boys looked at Webby, who glanced at Pow-Pow—still out of it—then nodded. All at once, the boys threw the dodgeballs at me! All of them!

"Hey!" I screamed. "I'm out!!!!"

Mr. Powell didn't do anything to stop it. I don't know why. He kept looking at his phone.

When Gilbert caught one of the balls, he reared back like he was really going to heave it at me. But then he stopped.

"Throw it, Mellencamp!" Webby yelled.

Yucky Gilbert clutched the ball to his chest and shook his head.

"Wuss," Webby spat out.

He picked up a ball and smashed it at me.

Luckily he was so obvious about it, I was able to dodge the dodgeball.

Ha.

Webby didn't like that at all.

Before he could get his hands on another ball, I called out Mr. Powell's name again, to get his attention.

Pow-Pow held up one finger. "I'll be right back, kids. I have to take this important call. Everybody hang tight." He ran out of the room. He left me there, all alone, with all those boys.

One of the balls rolled on the floor. Henry reached down to get it. I gave him my most pleading puppy-dog look: *Please, Henry, don't pummel me. I'm your oldest friend!*

"Get her, Henry," Webby ordered.

You know Henry pretty well, Bess. What do you think he did?

If you guessed *He pummeled Claire*, then you know him better than I do.

This story is making me feel so sad I have to take a break. I'll finish writing to you about the rest of the day after supper. We're having crabs and corn, last of the season. Bet you don't have that out in San Francisco.

Or maybe you do.

Later tater,
Claire

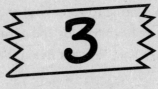

Poison Pizza

Hi Bess,

My story, continued:

After gym we had lunch. Pizza Day.

Okay, I thought. *Pizza is never bad*.

I went to the cafeteria and got in line. I got my pizza and salad and looked for a place to sit. Henry was sitting with Webby and his friends. I didn't want to sit anywhere near them, not after what happened in gym. But the cafeteria was pretty full.

And noisy. Food was flying everywhere. The second graders were singing "Row, Row, Row Your Boat" in burps.

For one happy second I imagined myself somewhere, anywhere else. I imagined myself at your new school— flowers on the tables, girls calling other girls over to sit with them and talk about what happened at the most recent slumber party, sharing cupcakes and cookies with each other, maybe even getting up to teach each other dance moves.

That's what it's like at your school, isn't it, Bess? If it isn't, I don't want to know.

There was room at the first graders' table, but when I went over there, Gabe gave me the stink eye. I guess he was embarrassed to have his big sister sit with him at lunch. The only other table with any room was next to Webby's. It was full of fourth graders.

I put my tray down. A fourth grader scowled at me.

(By the way, whenever I refer to any person at school, any fellow student, assume it is a boy. Because it is a boy. Remember, I am THE ONLY GIRL.)

"Why don't you go sit with your own grade?" the fourth grader said.

"No room," I told him. I made myself tall so he would get a good sense of my fifth-grade superiority. He backed down.

But then I realized I'd forgotten to get milk. I went to the drink station to get it. When I got back to my table, the fourth graders snickered. That made me suspicious.

I scanned my tray for signs of sabotage, but everything looked okay. I sat down.

I picked up my pizza and took a bite.

My mouth felt like it was on fire.

Someone had doused my slice in hot sauce. *Tons* of hot sauce.

It looks just like tomato sauce, so I didn't notice until it was too late.

I spat out the pizza. The fourth graders laughed and looked over at the table next to us. Webby's table.

"Who put hot sauce on my pizza?" I demanded.

They all cracked up. Somebody shouted, "Smuggler Joe did it!"

Sure. Whenever something goes wrong, Smuggler Joe did it.

Smuggler Joe spray-painted *Class of 2015 Rocks* on the water tower.

Smuggler Joe stole Mrs. Grimes's cat.

Smuggler Joe made Webby late for his sister's wedding.

Smuggler Joe haunts the old bait and tackle shop.

Smuggler Joe cut Mr. Pitovsky's boat loose.

Smuggler Joe sends flashlight signals to his ghost buddies across the river.

And now he put hot sauce on my pizza.

Uh-huh.

The boys in my class were laughing even harder than the fourth graders.

"Tell me!" I shouted. "Who did it?"

Webby pulled a little glass bottle out of his jacket pocket and wagged it at me.

Tabasco Sauce. Half empty.

I sprang to my feet.

"You ruined my lunch!" I tried to grab the bottle from Webby, but he tossed it to Zach M. I lunged for it, spilling Henry's milk. Mrs. Grimes stormed over and coughed twice. Then she growled, "What's all the commotion?"

"Claire attacked me!" Webby shrieked.

That little liar!

"I did not!" I said. "He tried to poison me!"

Mrs. Grimes stared me down. "I don't see any poison. But I did see you run over to this table in a fury and knock over a carton of milk."

She marched to the wall and wrote my name on the Bad Board!

Only MY name. Not Webby's or Henry's or anyone else's.

It's so unfair.

So I had detention after school. It was the first day of school. Nobody else had detention. There hadn't been time for anybody to do anything bad. Except me, of course.

Detention is in Ms. Ruiz's room this year. I sat alone in the classroom with her. I didn't have anything to do, not even homework. Mr. Harper let us off easy for the first day.

Ms. Ruiz sat at her desk reading a *Star Time* magazine. I read the graffiti kids had scratched into the desk where I sat. I stared out the window. I saw Henry and Webby ride off somewhere on their bikes.

I think Ms. Ruiz felt sorry for me, so she read some of the juicier celebrity gossip out loud.

"Did you know Taylor Swift loves red cotton socks?"

I told her that, no, I didn't know that.

"Listen to this—Kim Kardashian has a secret twin. They were separated at birth!"

To which I said: "Oh wow."

I was supposed to stay for an hour, but she let me go fifteen minutes early.

"Don't let the boys get you down," she told me as I was leaving. "Stay strong, sister." She's nice, Ms. Ruiz.

Still, Mom and Dad got mad at me when I came home late. After I explained, they said they understood. Mom said she'd talk to Mr. Unitas about being more sensitive about my situation.

I'm afraid talking to the principal is not going to be enough. Things are bad without you, Bess. It's going to be a long year.

LT,
C

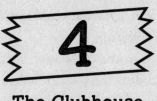

The Clubhouse

Bess,

Welcome to Day Two.

Last year, the best thing about being the only two girls in school was having the girls' bathroom all to ourselves. Our beloved clubhouse.

Mr. Jones painted it over the summer, so all of our drawings and poems from last year are gone. When I first walked in yesterday and saw those blank walls, it made me sad.

But then I thought: *New year, blank slate*. I can record the history of this year on the walls. Like cave paintings. Trouble is, there's no one around to see them but me. Being in our clubhouse without you makes me miss you the most.

Luckily I brought some things from home today to make the clubhouse cozy. I put a few of my favorite books on the shelf, next to the extra paper towels. Mom made me a pretty blue cushion just the right size for the windowsill, so now there's a window seat! I can sit there and read during free periods. I brought pictures of Bruno and Starshine and taped them to the walls. I drew frames around the pictures—a red frame with flowers around Bruno, a blue frame with stars for Starshine.

Instead of subjecting myself to the gross cafeteria again, I ate lunch in the clubhouse. I finished my sandwich and started drawing pictures on the wall to record the history of my first day of fifth grade. I drew a picture of me getting bombarded by balls in the gym. I called it "The Dodgeball Massacre." I made Webby look evil, with long, sharp teeth, snarling as he hurled a ball at me. I drew a halo around my head, like an angel.

I know I'm not an angel, but it's my cave and I can make the paintings any way I like. And it's not like anyone else will ever see them, except Mr. Jones, and I don't think he even looks at the walls while he's mopping the floors and restocking the toilet paper. At least, he's never said anything to me.

Then I drew the lunch incident: "Poison Pizza." It had two parts. Part 1: I'm gagging from the hot sauce. Part 2: I'm getting scolded by Mrs. Grimes for attacking Webby. Unfair.

Once the drawing was done, I sat on the window seat and looked around the bathroom. It's a very nice clubhouse, but a club with only one member isn't much fun.

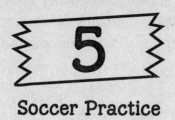

Soccer Practice

The rest of the afternoon was fairly calm. We had math and social studies. Then three-thirty came. Soccer practice.

I'm excited because this year our team gets to play against other schools. I really, really want to play center forward. Center forward is my spot. I love to kick those arching shots into the goal. I love the feel of the ball smacking against my right foot.

As you know, I was the high scorer on the team last year. Any sane coach would let me be center forward.

We don't have a sane coach, though. We have Pow-Pow.

Webby told Pow-Pow that *he* wanted to play center forward. Pow-Pow said, "Cool, I'll watch you and Claire during practice and assign positions to everyone next week." Henry's got halfback sewn up, and Yucky Gilbert wants to be goalie. Nobody else wants to be goalie, so the job is his.

You know how there's always a giant mud puddle in front of the goal whenever it rains? Well, it rained yesterday. Gilbert stepped right through the puddle and huddled in front of the net. By the end of practice, he was covered in mud and yuckier than ever.

The whole field was muddy—the mud spattered all over my legs as I ran. We started scrimmaging. I intercepted the ball. I was headed for the goal when Webby ran in front of me and tripped me—right in front of the giant mud puddle. I fell into it face-first.

Pow-Pow blew his whistle. Webby laughed. He tripped me on purpose! Anybody could see that. I waited for Pow-Pow to give him a penalty or at least yell at him, but he didn't say a word. He just asked if I was okay. I said, "Webby tripped me!"

Pow-Pow looked at Webby. Webby shrugged and said, "I didn't mean to."

I looked at Henry and said, "You saw him, right?"

Henry used to take my side against Webby all the

time. But not this time. He shrugged like Webby and said, "I didn't do anything."

"Long as nobody's hurt." Pow-Pow helped me up. Then he blew his whistle and shouted, "Resume play!"

We started playing again, and this time I swiped the ball from Webby, even though we were on the same team. *Shrieeeek!* went Pow-Pow's whistle. "Claire Warren! You don't sabotage a teammate!"

A few minutes later, Webby stole the ball from me—just like I did to him. Only somehow Pow-Pow didn't see it this time. Webby scored a goal, and Pow-Pow said, "Nice job, Webby."

I wanted to take a big handful of mud and rub it in Webby's face.

After practice, I wiped the mud off my legs and changed. I couldn't take a shower, because I don't have one. I have to change in the clubhouse. They turned the girls' locker room into Pow-Pow's private office. I guess he figured, since there's only one of me, I don't need a locker room all to myself. He probably likes having an office with his own shower in it.

Tonight at dinner, Mom asked, "How was school today, kids?"

Gabe gushed about how much he loves his teacher and how great it is that there are no girls in his class. I said that's exactly what I *don't* like about school this year.

24

Then Jim, Mr. Big Shot High School, showed Gabe how to make spitballs and spit them through straws at a target. The target being me.

"Mom!" I cried. "Jim and Gabe spit this at me!" I peeled a spitball off my forehead.

"It wasn't us," Jim said. "Smuggler Joe did it."

"No spitballs," Mom said, but she laughed at the Smuggler Joe thing.

Even at home I'm the only girl. Except for Mom, and she doesn't count.

It was still light out after dinner. I wished I could go visit you at your house, like I used to. But I couldn't, so I saddled up Starshine and went for a ride. Bruno came along. He likes to trot beside me and Starshine, wagging his tail and barking at squirrels.

We rode over to Eliot Point to look at the water. It calms me down to watch the sun set over the river. While we rode, I sang Starshine's special song to him.

I don't think I ever told you about Starshine's special song. I haven't told anyone, so the fact that I'm telling you now, IN WRITING, is proof that you are my closest friend.

You could probably guess the song if you think about it. It's "Good Morning, Starshine"! Mom used to sing it to me every morning when she woke me up. She still does sometimes, when she's in a sunny morning mood. I sing it to Starshine even when it's not morning, because I named him after the song. I can tell he likes it because his ears twitch in time when I sing it to him.

25

Now that you're gone, I guess Starshine and Bruno are my best friends.

Stupid Henry.

Miss you,
Claire

Swifty Surprise

Dear Bess,

Sorry I haven't written since last week. The rest of the week at school was more of the same, only worse, and I didn't want to bore you. Your school sounds like heaven. You really have milk and cookies every afternoon? And so many sports teams! I'm jealous. That girl you mentioned, Anna, sounds nice.

The big news here is the fall regatta, of course. It's two weeks away, and I haven't found a crew to replace you yet. I was going to ask Henry. I figured he'd be flattered to be asked to crew for the captain of the boat that won last spring.

☆ ☆ ☆ Yeah! Go, us! ☆ ☆ ☆

Everybody knows *Swifty* is the fastest 420 on the island and you and I are the fastest junior team anybody can remember. Since we broke every record last year, I thought those dumb boys would line up to crew for me this year. I'm scared to ask Henry, with the way he's been acting. I'm afraid he'll say no, even though he'd be crazy to turn me down. Doesn't he want to win?

Listen to this: Yesterday after school I went out back to the dock to get *Swifty* rigged up for a sail. She'd been covered up all week because of the rain and because I haven't had much time for sailing since school started.

I thought I heard a funny noise when I got close to the boat, kind of like a thump. I didn't think too much about it.

When I got closer to the boat, the tarp looked funny. Just off a little bit, not tied tightly.

My heart was beating fast. A tingle in my bones told me something wasn't right.

I ran into the house. "Mom! I think someone is hiding in *Swifty*!"

Mom wasn't immediately convinced. "What does this intruder look like?" she asked.

"I don't know," I told her. "I'm afraid to peek under the tarp."

"Maybe it's Smuggler Joe!"

Not funny.

"He's not real," I said.

"Sure he's real. A real ghost, anyway."

I didn't know whether she was teasing me or not.

"What's he doing hiding in my boat?" I asked.

"I expect he's taking a nap. Let's go out and see."

She was definitely teasing me.

We crept outside. The tarp still looked lumpy. It moved!

I grabbed Mom. She gasped and jumped back a foot.

"Ghosts don't make lumps—do they?" I said.

"Only one way to find out."

We stepped closer, quietly, quietly . . . The lump stayed still, but I could hear someone under there breathing, or more like panting.

"On three," Mom said. "Ready? One, two, three!"

I yanked off the tarp.

Bruno jumped up and licked my face.

"But it *could* have been Smuggler Joe," Mom said as we walked back to the house.

"What would we have done if it was?" I asked.

Mom shook her head. "I don't know. Asked him to come in for some iced tea?"

This seemed to me a rather friendly way to deal with a ghost thief. "Really?" I said. "But wouldn't he hurt us?"

"He'd never hurt a Foyes Islander. We're his people. Our ancestors hid the smugglers way back in the old days. They lived here among us, and when the government officers came looking for them, we'd just shrug and say, 'Joe? Never heard of him.'"

"How do you know all this?"

Mom smiled. "My parents told me, and their parents told them, and their parents told them . . ."

"Gotcha."

"In fact, people say he spent a lot of time at the Three Fiddlers Pub."

"The Three Fiddlers Pub? I never heard of that place."

"That's because it doesn't exist anymore. It was knocked down by one of the big hurricanes. But do you know where it once stood?"

"Where?"

"Right on this very spot."

Freaky, right?

"So Smuggler Joe used to hang out right here?" I asked.

"Well, we can't say for sure he was even real. But if he was, he would have been here. It was a smugglers' hangout."

Your family's not from the Island originally, Bess, so maybe you never heard those old stories. But you've heard of Smuggler Joe, of course. Because he—or his ghost—gets blamed for everything around here.

People like Mom talk about him as if he were a real person. But no one really knows if he was or wasn't. Sometimes I think he's just a legend, like Bigfoot. But who knows?

Not me. That's for sure.

Later tater,
Claire-ator

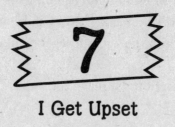

I Get Upset

Bess,

Today I finally asked Henry if he wants to crew for me in the regatta. Do you know what he said? You're not going to believe it. YOU ARE NOT GOING TO BELIEVE IT.

He said,

and I quote:

"I won't crew for a girl."

Then he walked away.

Does that sound like Henry to you? OUR Henry?

What happened to him?

Maybe he never actually liked me. Maybe he only hung out with me to be near you. Is that true? If that's true, you better tell me. Don't be afraid of hurting my feelings.

In a way, knowing that he never liked me would make me feel better. At least it would explain why he's acting so weird. The only other explanation I can think of is that he's possessed by a ghost who hates girls.

I'm sorry. I'm so upset I have to stop writing now.

I'll Show Everyone

Okay, I'm back.

After Henry turned me down I went into shock. I went numb. But when I wrote down what he said and saw his words in black and white . . . well, it hit me, really hit me. Henry might as well have slapped my face, that's how much it hurt.

I made a tent in my room, just like we used to do when you spent the night here. I tied a big blue sheet between the posts of my twin beds and made a tent. Then I sat on the rug between the beds and looked at how the sheet filtered the sunlight in my room and made everything in the tent look blue. My hands turned blue, and my arms, and my feet, even my toenails. Blue, blue, blue.

I felt sad for a long time. But then I started to get mad.

I'm the best junior sailor on Foyes Island, and Henry doesn't want to crew for me because I'm a girl?

Fine.

I'll show him.

I'll show everyone.

I'll win the regatta again this fall, two races in a row. And next spring too. Nobody's ever won three Foyes Island regattas in a row. I'll be the first. Girl or no girl.

The trouble is, I can't win all by myself. I need some-body to crew for me. I'll ask around tomorrow at school. The next best sailor after me and Henry is Webby, but I can't ask him. There's got to be somebody else.

Well, good night, Bess. I'll let you know what hap-pens tomorrow.

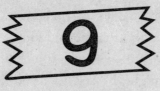

New Crew

I'm getting used to fifth grade now. It's been a few weeks. Mr. Harper's not bad. I wouldn't call him nice, exactly, but he tries to be fair. That's more than I can say for a lot of the other teachers at that school. (Pow-Pow, ahem ahem.)

My favorite part of school is hanging out in the clubhouse. I eat my lunch in there every day now, which sounds gross, but it's not. Nothing's grosser than an all-boy cafeteria during lunchtime. When I do set foot in there, I usually come out covered in bread crumbs or with smushed banana stuck to my shoe or something.

I eat fast, and then I read or draw on the walls. I'm reading *The Black Stallion*, which is really good, but not as good as *Misty of Chincoteague*. Misty reminds me of Starshine a little bit. The Black Stallion is a lot more fiery and noble than Starshine. I love Starshine but he pretty much lives to eat apples. He's not, like, a hero horse who rescues people or anything.

Every day I draw the sad story of my life on the walls. I drew my boat with Bruno popping out from under the tarp. I drew a picture of me in Starshine's stable, reading *The Black Stallion* to him.

Meanwhile, I have news about my crew for the regatta. Not good news. I asked every boy in the class—well, every boy except one. I would have done anything to avoid asking that one boy to crew for me. I even asked some fourth graders. They all said no. These boys, it's like they're in a cult or something and they can't have anything to do with a girl.

Finally I asked the boy who was my last resort. I don't have to tell you his name. I'm sure you can guess.

His initials are Y.G. And guess what.

He said yes.

I have to hand it to Gilbert. He might be the yuckiest person ever born, but he's the only boy who's willing to go against the other boys. Maybe the Webby boys don't want him around because he's so yucky. Oh well. Yucky Gilbert will be crewing for me at the regatta.

I know, I know. He's a terrible sailor. He has no sense of direction. We'll have to practice a lot, which only makes the whole thing worse. I told him I have a lot of rules on my ship, but the first and most important rule is: *No Slobbering.*

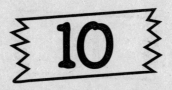

We Interrupt This Letter for a
Message from Yucky Gilbert

Dear Bess,

Gilbert here. How's California? Everyone misses you here on Foyes, but Claire misses you most of all, I think.

Did she tell you I'm going to crew for her? When she asked me I was so happy! She's the best sailor on the island! The best kid sailor, anyway. I've never won anything in my life, so I can't wait to finally win the regatta! If we win. Knock wood.

Here's the thing: I'm so nervous. I'm not as good a sailor as you. You won with Claire last year. That's why I'm writing to you—well, besides wanting to say hi and how are you and all that. Do you have any tips for me? What can I do to help our boat win? How can I keep Claire from getting mad at me? She's always yelling at me.

Thanks!

Your friend,
Gilbert

First Rule: No Slobbering

Dear Bess,

Gilbert and I took the boat out after school today. There was a stiff breeze from the south. The first time we tacked I called, "Ready about!" and he leaned over and tried to kiss me. The boom swung around and smacked us both into the water.

I bobbed up for air and spit out the water in my mouth. I screamed at him, "I told you the first rule is No Kissing!"

"No you didn't," he said. "You said the first rule is No Slobbering." And then he spit a long stream of water at me through his braces.

He's got nerve.

We climbed back aboard and tried again. The next time we went about he leaned too far over and we capsized. Good thing the water isn't cold yet. I spent the whole afternoon soaking wet.

"You're the worst crew who was ever born," I told him. I was clinging to the hull of *Swifty*, trying to figure out how we were going to push her right again.

"I think you're cute," Gilbert said.

That's his answer to everything.

Webby and Henry sped by on the *Hot Streak*. They saw *Swifty* bobbing upside down in the water and pointed and laughed at us as they zoomed by.

"Wow, they're really going fast," Gilbert said. "I don't see how we'll ever beat them."

I wanted to leave him floating in his life jacket out in the middle of the inlet and let him swim to shore by himself. I GUESS he knows how to swim. But I needed him to help me tow *Swifty* back to the dock so we could bail her out and set her right again.

I have a bad feeling about this, Bess. I'm telling you.

Wish you were here,
Claire

Bathroom Invasion

Dear Bess,

Everyone kept saying I'd get used to being the only girl in school. "Give it a few weeks," they said. "After a while you won't even notice the difference between you and the boys."

It's been over a month, and I still notice the difference. I hear the boys horsing around without me in their locker room after gym. They have all these in-jokes and signals that I don't understand. Say Zach M. makes a V with his fingers and points it at Webby and Webby nods meaningfully. If I ask, "What does that mean?" they laugh and say, "It's a guy thing."

Except that, whatever it is, I'm pretty sure it's not a guy thing. Probably it's just a stupid thing.

I miss you more than ever. I wear the Neptune necklace you gave me every day. It's great writing to you and video-chatting but I wish you were here to live through these school days with me. I wish you were here so you would know exactly how I feel and exactly what I'm talking about. Sometimes Jim says I'm whining, like, "So you're the only girl, what's the big deal? Boys are more fun anyway."

Sometimes I hate Jim.

I'M LONELY and I MISS YOU. And I'M MAD. Because the one thing I had for myself, my one safe place in the whole school, was our bathroom clubhouse. Every day I draw on the wall, a little scene of something that happened to me.

But now somebody's invaded our clubhouse!

I was out sick yesterday, and today when I got to school I went to the clubhouse first thing. I felt right away that something was wrong. I scanned the room until I spotted it.

Somebody had drawn something on the wall! With markers.

Permanent markers.

It wasn't a good drawing either. It was kind of a cartoon of me—you could tell it was me because, first of all, it was a girl, so who else could it be? She was wearing the Foyes Island soccer uniform, and she had a long brown braid like mine. Without the braid, actually, you could hardly tell it was a person. It might have been a cat. That's how bad the drawing was.

So what? you might say. *So someone drew a picture of you in your soccer uniform. That doesn't sound so bad.*

I know. But that's not all. The picture showed me falling down in a big muddle puddle. With an action bubble that said SPLAT! Which is exactly what happened on the

43

first day of soccer practice. I drew my own version of it!
I'm not sure the invader even noticed that. Mine didn't
say SPLAT! though.

It's humiliating. And it is not what really happened
that day.

Webby is the one who tripped me. That's why I'm
99.99999% sure WEBBY is the one who broke into the
girls' bathroom and drew on my wall!!!!

I HATE WEBBY!!!!!!!!!!

I told Mr. Unitas that some boy went into the girls'
bathroom and drew on the wall.

"How do you know it wasn't a girl?" he asked.

I stared at him for a second and he took it back.

"My mistake." Then he couldn't help it. He just had
to add, "Maybe it was Smuggler Joe!"

I gave him a look, like, *Don't toy with me.*

"Well, who do you think did it?" he asked, more serious now.

"I have a theory but I don't know for sure."

"I don't want to hear your theories. But if you have any proof do let me know."

I said I'd get back to him.

I'm going to set a trap in the bathroom and catch Webby in the act. And then I'm going to get my revenge. I'm researching bathroom traps right now. I'll let you know when I figure out how to do it.

LT,
Claire

13

Race Day

Well, Bess, today was the day. Regatta Day. I could tell you how I finished the race now and save you the suspense. I know how you hate being kept in suspense. But I'm not going to spare you! No. Bwa ha ha! You have to read through this entire thing to find out what happened! Trust me, it's better that way.

Yesterday I scrubbed *Swifty*'s hull till it sparkled, then I went to bed early for a good night's sleep. I made sure to wear the Neptune necklace you gave me for good luck.

This morning I woke up early. Bruno woke me, licking my face till I sat up. I think he was afraid I'd oversleep and miss the race.

It was dark out, with big gray clouds looming over the horizon and a stiff easterly breeze. One of those days that feel like a storm's coming all day long. It doesn't come and it doesn't come and the tension builds up and you're just waiting for it. Then finally it comes, the clouds open up or a bolt of lightning splits them open and everybody runs for cover.

But I'm getting ahead of myself.

I went into the kitchen and poured myself some cereal. Dad came in a little while later and started making pancakes. We were all racing, except Gabe. Dad was crewing for Uncle Eddie on the 14, and Jim was crewing for Mom.

You know what race day is like at our house. Everybody was quiet. The only sound in the kitchen was chewing. Even Bruno chewed. I think chewing is a gross sound—*smack smack smack*—so I tried not to listen. When Dad got up to clear the table he said, "You ready for your race today, Claire?"

"Ready as I'll ever be," I said gloomily. I didn't feel ready at all.

"You, Tessie?" Dad asked Mom.

"We're good and ready," she answered. "You and Eddie better watch yourselves."

Mom patted Jim on the back.

"Long as somebody beats Lloyd Peterson," Dad said.

"And Webby," I chimed in.

My dad nodded. "Both father *and* son. They're going down. I don't care who takes them down, as long as they don't win this thing."

Mom laughed. "I know you, John Warren. You want to win bad as ever. You want to beat all of us. Even your own wife and son."

"All right, I admit it. I want to beat the pants off you two. But I do hope you'll come in second. Does that make you feel better?"

"I'll wave to you from the finish line, Dad," Jim said.

"Son, your mom's a crack sailor, but I know all her tricks."

"I know all yours too, John," Mom pointed out.

"Not all of them. Claire, you show that Peterson boy what the Warrens are made of."

"I'll do my best, Dad," I promised.

What else could I say? With Gilbert as my crew, I figured we had no chance. Okay, a tiny chance. But only if he didn't punch a hole in the bottom of the boat or steer us to China. Which he was 98.8% likely to do.

Dad loaded *Swifty* onto his trailer and we piled into the car and drove to the marina. Oxford Road was a parade of cars and pickups, all headed to the inlet. People were hanging out the car windows, yelling and hooting and hollering.

Gilbert was waiting for me in the junior clubhouse. He handed me a plastic cup full of some kind of thick green liquid.

"What is this gunk?" I asked him.

"Kale smoothie," he said. "For energy. Drink up."

"No way." I almost tossed the drink on the ground and threw the cup away. But then I pictured how it would look like an alien had barfed on the parking lot. Plus, I sensed I would need the extra energy. I wasn't dying to drink alien barf, but I shut my eyes, tilted my head back, and gulped it down quick before I could taste it.

Yeee-ech.

When I opened my eyes, Gilbert was grinning hopefully at me. "Not bad, right?"

"Not good," I said. "Come on. Let's go." Gilbert helped me and Dad pull *Swifty* to the launch. We rigged her up.

There were eight boats competing in the twelve-and-unders this year. Webby's tough but you should see Harold Beame. This is his last year in the twelve-and-unders, thank goodness—he looks about seventeen. Mom says he hit puberty early. He's about five eleven and already shaving, with shoulders as broad as I am tall. Jake Weiss was his crew, and he's pretty big now too. He had a growth spurt over the summer.

"Hey, punk," Harold said to me. "You're not going to win this year. Just letting you know now so you won't be disappointed later."

"We are too going to win!" Gilbert piped up. I threw him a sharp look that meant *Please don't talk*, but I don't think he got the message.

"That's what you said last spring, Harold," I said.

"Last spring was a fluke. Last spring I didn't have these." Harold flexed his new biceps, which look like baked potatoes. "And that's a pretty hefty breeze out there."

He was right—the wind was coming strong out of the east, and it takes more strength to handle a boat in a strong wind. The wind was pretty light last year when we won. I hated it when people said we won because we were the lightest boat. First of all, that isn't true: There were three boats with skinny little boy teams who were lighter than us. Second of all, it doesn't matter how

49

little you weigh—if you can't sail, you're not going to win a race.

Maybe I'm not as strong as Harold and Jake, but I'm smarter than both of them put together, even if you subtract Gilbert's brains.

But Webby's smart too. Not just smart: Crafty. Sneaky. And he had Henry in his boat. Henry, who has sailed with me since we first learned how. Henry, who knows all my tricks, just like Dad knows all Mom's tricks. Webby and Henry were rigging the *Hot Streak*, listening to Harold and me and not saying anything.

Mr. Peeler—he's the fleet captain this year—called us together to go over the rules of the race:

Sail out past the second buoy, the red one in the middle of the river, and back, three times.

No cheating.

"The committee boat will be watching," he said.

Gilbert and I left *Swifty* alone for a few minutes to hear Mr. Peeler's instructions—just five minutes. But that was enough.

We returned to our boats to start the race. I rechecked the riggings, and Gilbert and I launched *Swifty* into the water. She felt a little heavy, but I didn't think much about it.

We sailed around the first buoy once. The dark clouds kept rolling in. It was really windy. Almost too windy, I thought. I was having a hard time keeping the mainsail in line. When we zipped past the committee boat, I felt like I was going to blow away.

But they didn't cancel the race. Kevin and Zach R. capsized before we even started. They righted themselves pretty fast, but they were the last to cross the starting line and they never caught up to the rest of us. Kevin was screaming at Zach, who looked like a wet raccoon.

The *Hot Streak* crossed the starting line first. Gilbert and I were right behind them. Then Harold and Jake passed us. It was pretty much our three boats the whole race. I ordered Gilbert around and he did everything right. We were riding back in a close third, so I told him to pull in the jib to give us a little speed—*Swifty* felt sluggish. We couldn't catch Webby. I didn't get it. In practice we could usually catch him in a strong wind. But not now.

"Something feels wrong," I told Gilbert.

He shrugged and said, "You're the boss."

Not very helpful.

I wished you were there. You would have sniffed the air with that bloodhound nose of yours and found the problem right away. Nobody sniffs out evildoing like you, Bess.

Two circuits round the buoy and we were stuck in third and falling behind. The wind was dying, so we should have been pulling ahead, since we were lighter than the other teams. I kept wondering what was wrong. *Maybe the jib has a hole in it*, I thought. I crawled up to check and my foot hit something under the bow. There wasn't supposed to be anything there. I bent down and found . . .

Two sacks of potatoes stuffed way up under the bow and hidden under a couple of extra life jackets!!!!

Who could have put them there?

(I'm asking sarcastically, of course.)

I yelled to Gilbert and pointed out the sacks. "Throw them overboard!" I ordered. I took the tiller while he threw the potatoes into the water. Right away we sped up. It felt like an engine had kicked in.

"All right!" I shouted. "Now we're cooking!"

We pulled up alongside the *Hot Streak*. Webby was screaming his head off at Henry, telling him to let out the jib, then pull it back in, lean out, trim the mainsail, anything to stop us.

I hope Henry enjoyed being yelled at.

Just as we were pulling ahead, Webby tacked in front of us from the left—he tried to cut us off! We almost collided. I yanked the tiller and we just missed them.

"Nice try, cheaters!" I called to them.

"Yeah, eat brackish water!" Gilbert yelled.

I looked at him. "Eat what?"

He shrugged again. He's always shrugging. It's a terrible habit.

The only boat ahead of us now was Harold and Jake's boat, *Godzilla*. The wind was really easing up, so we glided along on top of the water, light as can be, and they were lumbering like . . . well, like a big lizard. I saw the committee boat ahead and the finish line just past it.

Mom and Dad and Gabe and Jim were on the shore, yelling and screaming, "Come on, *Swifty*! Go, Claire!"

Gilbert pulled in the mainsail just a little and we sped past *Godzilla* and over the finish line in first place.

Yeah, that's right, Bessie! *Swifty* won again! That's two races in a row.

Here's a picture of me and Gilbert with the trophy:

Of course, you know what the trophy looks like, since we won it last spring. Your name is inscribed right under mine on the cup. I wished so hard that you were there instead of Gilbert. I would have given you the biggest, happiest hug. Instead, I had to hug my mom and dad. No way was I going to hug Gilbert, even if he did hold out his arms like he was waiting for it. He also jumped up and down, shrieking, "We won! We won!"

I kissed the Neptune charm on my necklace. It was the next best thing to having you there.

Godzilla came in second. Webby and Henry had to settle for third. Cheaters.

I would have reported them for cheating, but I had no proof. *Somebody* put those potatoes in our boat, and we almost lost the race because of it. I'm pretty sure it was Webby. It could have been Harold and Jake, but frankly, I doubt they're smart enough to think of a prank like that.

There's not much I can do without proof.

I just have to catch Webby at something else . . .

Your race partner forever,
Claire

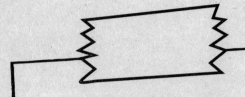

Part 2

The Ghost of Foyes Island

November

Holiday Play

Dear Bess,

Guess what? They announced the holiday play. It's *A Christmas Carol*. Mr. Harper is the drama teacher this year and he told me if I want to be in the play I don't even have to try out. They picked *A Christmas Carol* because all the main parts are for boys. Mr. H. said I can have any of the female parts I want. I can even play all of them if I can handle it.

I want to play Scrooge. I told him that.

Mr. Harper sighed and looked at me like I was the Ghost of Christmas Never.

"Okay," he hemmed. Then he hawed, "But if you want to play Scrooge, you'll have to audition."

I thought about taking the girl parts. Because if I don't, I'm not sure anyone else will, except maybe a teacher. It's not fair—but this whole year is unfair, right?

The girl parts are:

Scrooge's sister, Fan
His girlfriend, Belle

Old Mrs. Fezziwig
Mrs. Cratchit
Scrooge's housekeeper
Scrooge's nephew Fred's wife
And the Ghost of Christmas Past, maybe

The Ghost of Christmas Past is the most interesting part, and it could go either way. Mr. Harper said they might give that part to a boy if they don't have enough boy roles to go around.

So I get to be married three times, I get to have a lame brother and a horrible boyfriend, AND I get to clean up after the meanest boss who ever lived. All in one hour.

That's a lot for one girl.

But I figure it's not worth the trouble auditioning for Scrooge. He's an old man, so it's easier to give the role to a boy.

And he's a jerk. So there are plenty of boys in my class who could play him really well.

You know who I mean.

And if I'm being honest, there's also the real reason: When it comes to acting, I'm not that great. I like being in plays, but it's not my dream to be an actress or anything. My audition is not going to blow everybody's mind and make Mr. Harper say, *Girl or no girl, the part of Scrooge must be played by Claire!*

A few of the boys are way better actors than me, so let them play the lead. I'm happy being the two-time junior regatta champion.

I can't be a genius at everything.

15

Stinky Scrooge

Mr. Harper held auditions during recess today. I went to the auditorium to watch. Most of the boys tried out for Scrooge. Mr. Harper explained how they can't ALL play Scrooge. Only one of them can, and there won't be a play unless some people play the other parts.

It didn't matter what he said. They all wanted to be the star.

Mr. Harper noticed me sitting in the audience and asked if I'd read with the wannabes. We did the scene where Bob Cratchit comes to work a little late on the day after Christmas and he doesn't know that Scrooge has turned good. Scrooge wants to play a joke on Bob Cratchit, so he pretends to be mean. He scares Bob, and then laughs and says that he has seen the error of his old mean ways and wants to be nice now.

Mr. Harper said he chose that scene because it shows both Scrooges, Nice Scrooge and Mean Scrooge. I read Bob Cratchit's part. I read it over and over again, with each boy who wanted to play Scrooge.

Honestly, none of the boys were that great. Kevin

and Zach M. were terrible! Totally flat. Gilbert was too mousy—his Bad Scrooge seemed kind of nice.

Webby was good as Mean Scrooge, but his Nice Scrooge was totally unconvincing. Further proof, if we needed any, that Webby doesn't have a nice bone in his body.

Henry was the best. It was fun reading with him. Once we started playing our parts, he loosened up and seemed like my old friend Henry again, funny and warm and nice. But as soon as the scene was over he went back to being too cool. He sat down next to Webby, his new best friend, and ignored me.

Good luck with that, Henry. Some friend Webby is.

Will Webby make you chocolate chip cookies when you're sick?

Doubtful.

Will he laugh when you tell one of your dumbest jokes ever?

He's way too cool to laugh at your jokes. The only jokes Webby laughs at are his own.

I drew a scene from the auditions on my clubhouse wall. It shows Webby on the stage trying to giggle and laugh like Nice Scrooge, saying "I'm light as a feather! I'm happy as a schoolboy!"—but instead of niceness, stink lines are coming off of him.

Mr. Harper is posting the cast list tomorrow.

All the boys are freaking out.

I guess I'm the only one who knows which parts she's going to get.

16

Later the Same Day . . .

Speaking of stink lines, soccer practice reeks.

Pow-Pow has been letting me play center forward most of the time, but he hasn't officially announced the positions yet. Webby's been playing left forward, but he keeps swerving over to the center, so the left side isn't covered. Once in a while Pow-Pow yells at him to get back to his position, but sometimes he doesn't.

Today during scrimmage, when Henry passed the ball to me to make a shot, Webby was out of his position and practically on top of me. He intercepted the ball, even though we were playing on the same team. It happened three times! And twice Webby scored goals. So Pow-Pow didn't yell at him, because he loves anything we do that scores a goal.

I told Webby to go back to his side of the field, and he punched me in the arm.

Yes. That's right.

PUNCHED ME IN THE ARM.

"Mr. Powell!" I shouted. "Webby punched me!"

Finally, I thought, *Webby will get in trouble.*

But what was Pow-Pow's reaction? He asked me, "Where?"

Like it matters where he punched me.

I showed him. He looked at my arm and said, "You'll live." To Webby he said, "Peterson, no punching."

And that was it.

Next time Pow-Pow wasn't looking, Webby punched me again!

"That's for being a tattletale," he said. "If you want to be one of us, you've got to take it like one of us."

Who ever said anything about wanting to be one of them?

Still I didn't tell on him this time. Because what good did it do?

Later, I saw Webby punch Henry in the arm too, after Henry took a shot that could have been Webby's.

It didn't make me feel much better. With Webby, you get punched if you're one of them and punched if you're not.

Now I've got a big blue bruise on my upper arm. Do you think I should show it to Pow-Pow? I don't want him to think I'm a baby and a tattletale just because I'm a girl. I'm as tough as Webby or any of those boys. I just like things to be fair.

Our biggest game of the season is coming up next week, against St. Anselm. Their team is all boys. They have a separate girls team. I heard Zach say to Webby that it's embarrassing that we have a girl on our team.

I think it's embarrassing that we have Webby.

Cast List and a Trap

Mr. Harper posted the cast list today. Here it is:

Ebenezer Scrooge: Henry Long
Scrooge as a boy: Calvin Pitovsky
Bob Cratchit: Gilbert Mellencamp
Marley's Ghost: Webster Peterson
Ghost of Christmas Past: Claire Warren
Ghost of Christmas Present: Kevin Ames
Ghost of Christmas Future: Webster Peterson
Tiny Tim: Zachary Mendoza
Fred: Zachary Roth
Mrs. Cratchit: Claire Warren
Fan: Claire Warren
Mrs. Fezziwig: Claire Warren
Belle: Claire Warren
Fred's wife: Claire Warren
Scrooge's housekeeper: Claire Warren

Looks like I have a lot of speedy costume changes in my future. Did you notice that he gave the two scariest roles to Webby? I think Mr. Harper sees right through Webby's freckled face into his dark sticky soul.

Also, he used Webby's real name. Which must've killed him. ☺

Meanwhile, I researched traps and think I found one that will work. I'm going to put baby powder on the floor near my wall drawings. If somebody steps near the wall, I'll get an impression of his shoe print. Then I can match Webby's shoes to the shoe print and prove he's the one who's been sneaking into my clubhouse and drawing on my wall!

It's time for a little justice around here.

18

Today in Soccer Horror

We were practicing penalty kicks—you know, running up to the ball and kicking it into the goal. Gilbert tried to block our kicks. I kicked the ball past him into the goal on my first two turns. Webby made it in once and once Gilbert caught his shot. On my third turn, Webby tripped me as I was running toward the ball. Pow-Pow told me to watch my footwork.

I think Webby's hoping I'll quit the team so he can play center. Well, if that's what he's waiting for, he's got a long wait ahead of him. I'm not quitting that team. No way.

19

A Ghost Gives Me an Idea

We had our first rehearsal for the play today. Most of my lines come when I'm the Ghost of Christmas Past. I fly Scrooge through the air to visit his childhood and show him scenes from his early life.

(I'm not really flying in the air. I'm actually standing behind some paper clouds on a red wagon that's pulled by a rope offstage.)

As soon as I've flown Scrooge back to his childhood, I have to slip offstage and change into Fan, Scrooge's beloved sister. I wear Fan's white dress underneath my Ghost robe, so all I have to do is take off the robe and put on a blond wig. (The wig, by the way, looks very familiar—like something a lunch lady would wear. I think Mr. Harper borrowed it from Mrs. Grimes. It smells like sloppy joes, and whenever I put it on, I get the urge to write names on the Bad Board. I really, REALLY hope Mrs. Grimes has never worn it.)

As Fan, I visit Boy Scrooge at school, where's he's very lonely. I have a long talk with him about our father and how he's ever so much nicer now than he used to be. Boy Scrooge cries tears of joy. Our father never liked him.

Scrooge doesn't understand why, but to me it's perfectly obvious—it's because Scrooge is an obnoxious jerk.

But I don't have time to make this point because (1) It's not in the script and (2) I have to hurry up and skip offstage (really, Mr. Harper is making me SKIP), take off the blond wig, put my Ghost robe back on, jump on the wagon, and be the Ghost of Christmas Past again.

If the audience is wondering why the Ghost of Christmas Past seems really sweaty, it's not my fault.

I say to Scrooge, "See, your sister adored you." (I say this in a special deep ghost voice so you can tell I'm not talking about . . . well, me.) "And now we visit another part of your past, when you were an apprentice for Mr. Fezziwig."

The scene changes to Mr. Fezziwig's Christmas party. I change into Mr. Fezziwig's wife. Fezziwig is Scrooge's boss, and for the office party, I'm wearing a white wig (which smells like mothballs and not sloppy joes, thank goodness) and a green dress.

This means I have exactly thirty seconds to change my dress in a curtained-off area that Ms. Ruiz and Ms. Teitelman are guarding.

Ms. Ruiz has to zip me up. At least Mr. Harper did not assign a BOY to zip me up. I'm grateful for the little things.

Then I put on my Ghost robe again. Then I'm back in the changing area, putting on a beautiful blue satin dress to play Belle, Scrooge's girlfriend. I give him back his engagement ring and say, "There's something you love more than me, Ebenezer: money."

Back to Ghost again. Then I have to be Fan one more time, this time with tummy padding, because I just had a baby. The baby is played by a doll who will grow up to be Zach R., who plays Fred, who will be my husband later, when I turn into Fred's Wife.

But before all that can happen, I have to die in childbirth. It's a very touching scene.

"Ebenezer," I whisper (loudly, because everyone needs to hear me), "promise me . . . promise me . . ."

And this is where it gets weird. Henry gives me this sad look, and it kind of breaks my heart. I know he looks sad because he's playing Scrooge and the script says that Scrooge is supposed to look sad when his beloved sister dies. But this Scrooge has Henry's face. And behind Scrooge's eyes are Henry's eyes, where I get a tiny glimpse of the nice old Henry, the Henry who liked me.

It only lasts a second, but it's there.

"Promise you what, Fan?" Scrooge asks.

"Promise me . . . you'll take care of my boy."

"Of course." Scrooge sobs and takes the baby doll in his arms. Then I die.

I don't stay dead long, though. The lights go out, I stand up and rip off the sloppy joe wig, someone puts my Ghost robe on again, the lights go on, and I'm standing over Scrooge, saying, "You heard her, Ebenezer. But you didn't take care of your nephew, did you?"

It's exhausting. But it did give me an idea.

Henry-as-Scrooge watches all these scenes from his past and feels bad about how hard-hearted he's gotten. If it worked for Scrooge, maybe it will work on Henry.

Here's my plan:

I'm going to scare Henry into being friends with me again.

How, you ask? That's for me to know and you to find out later . . . after I figure it out.

Miss you,
C

20

A Clue, and a Problem

Dear Bess,

I found my first clue! This morning, in the clubhouse. I left baby powder on the floor, and now there's a footprint!

Nothing else happened—nobody drew on my wall or did any other damage to the clubhouse. Still, if that footprint matches Webby's, I'VE CAUGHT HIM.

It's an awfully big footprint, though.

I snapped a photo of the footprint. When I went to class I sneaked a glance at Webby's feet. He was wearing his usual sneakers. The footprint looks like a sneaker print too. I need one of his shoes to match against the print.

But how to get it?

Soccer practice, that's how. He has to change from normal sneakers to cleats. We all do. The problem is, stealing his shoe from the boys' locker room, taking it to the clubhouse, measuring it, photographing it, and sneaking it back to Webby's locker will not be easy. It will also make me late for practice. I'm already on Pow-Pow's bad side. I can't make things worse.

If I get caught, Pow-Pow will get mad. He might get so mad he'll kick me off the team.

But that's a chance I'll have to take in my quest for justice.

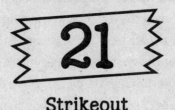

Strikeout

I lucked out. Webby took off his shoes in art class today. We were making a banner on a long roll of paper to decorate the halls for the holiday season. The banner says PEACE ON EARTH, and Mr. Strickland asked us to make handprints on the banner. Webby decided to make footprints instead. Mr. Strickland frowned but he let it go in the name of peace on earth.

Webby took off his sneakers. While he was splashing around in blue paint, I nabbed one of his shoes and dipped the sole in paint. Then I made an impression of it on a piece of paper. I felt very clever.

When class was over, Webby put his sneakers back on. He didn't even notice that the bottom of the left one was blue. He walked to the door, leaving one blue footprint behind him. Mr. Strickland stopped him.

"Webby, I think you stepped in some paint."

"Did not," Webby said.

"Oh yeah? Lift up your foot."

Webby lifted his right foot, which was clean. "See? Told you."

"No, your other foot."

Webby lifted up his left foot, which was blue on the bottom. He frowned. Mr. Strickland told him to take it off and clean it before he tracked paint all over the school. I sneaked out of the room with my evidence while Webby grumbled about having to clean up a mess he didn't make. Tee hee hee.

I went straight to the clubhouse to check Webby's footprint against the one in the baby powder. The baby powder one was fading a bit, but I could tell right away that Webby's didn't match.

It was too small.

As I left the clubhouse I spotted Mr. Jones, the janitor, mopping up the hallway. I couldn't help noticing he was wearing sneakers. He stepped on the wet floor and I saw the print his shoe made.

It looked familiar.

Mr. Jones made the footprint. Not Webby.

Mr. Jones had come into the clubhouse to clean it, I guess. Or to replace the paper towels or the toilet paper.

Oh well.

My first trap didn't work. I'll have to think of another one.

Your disappointed friend,
C

22

Even My Own Mother Is Against Me

Dear Bess,

We rehearsed for the holiday play this afternoon. This time we worked on scenes from Scrooge's Christmas Future. I play Mrs. Cratchit. I have to sit rocking by the fireplace, crying over Tiny Tim and burbling over his sweet little crutch by the hearth. Zach M. plays Tiny Tim. I found it hard to cry over him.

Maybe I should have tried out for Scrooge after all.

Tomorrow is our big game against St. Anselm. Everybody's very nervous about it. Pow-Pow worked us really hard in practice today. Before he let us go he gave us a big pep talk.

"Kids, people will tell you that it's not whether you win or lose, it's how you play the game," he said. "Well, I strongly disagree with that sentiment. If you play the game right, you should win! Face it, winning is all that matters. You know it, I know it, your parents know it, and most important, the other team knows it. If you lose, Turtles, I'm here to tell you you'll feel terrible about yourselves afterward. And we don't want to feel bad, do we?"

Everybody looked kind of confused. I think we were all afraid this was some kind of trick question.

"Do we?" he asked again.

"No?" Webby and a few other boys said.

"I can't hear you! DO WE WANT TO FEEL LIKE LOSERS?"

"No!" we shouted.

I was kind of surprised to hear Pow-Pow say these things out loud. I figured he *thought* them, secretly, but I didn't think he'd actually admit to it.

"Now, I've got to warn you," Pow-Pow went on. "The St. Anselm boys are bigger than you all, and a lot of them have had more experience than you. They've played on travel teams and whatnot since they were knee-high to a jellyfish. St. A.'s is a big school. They have lots of kids to choose from for their sports teams. You actually have to try out to make the team. They don't have to take everybody who wants to play, like we do."

Maybe it was my imagination, but I could swear Pow-Pow was looking at me when he said that. Me, last year's high scorer. It really burned my bacon.

Then he assigned us our positions for the game tomorrow. Webby got center forward. I got left forward.

My bacon was burned super-crispy.

"Yes!" Webby jumped up and raised his arms in triumph. "Justice is done!" Then he looked at me to see how I felt about this. Maybe he expected me to cry or something. If so, I disappointed him.

"See you on the field" was all I said.

But inside, I was stewing. There's no doubt about it: Pow-Pow hates me.

When I got home from school, Mom asked me to help her with dinner because Dad was out on the boat and she was busy with a work deadline.

I looked around the kitchen. Was I the only kid in the house? No, I was not. Gabe was drawing at the kitchen table, and Jim's backpack was lying in the middle of the floor, where he had no doubt left it on his way upstairs.

"Why don't you ask Jim to help?" I asked. "He's older."

"Because he's got a lot of homework to do," Mom answered.

"You mean, because he's a boy," I pointed out.

Mom did not like this answer. "No, that's not what I mean, and stop looking for discrimination everywhere. Sometimes it's just not there."

Easy for her to say. She wasn't the only girl at work.

"But sometimes it is," I said, thinking of Pow-Pow and Webby.

Mom sighed and softened—but only a little.

"Okay, yeah, sometimes it is," she said. "Now would you please wash this lettuce?"

Jim got to stay in his room.

But don't worry. He had to clean the dishes after dinner. And I made sure mine was extra dirty.

Sloppily yours,
C

23

Gorillas vs. Turtles

Dear Bess,

Today was so exciting! Here's the blow-by-blow:

The Foyes Island Turtles played the St. Anselm Gorillas after school. The Gorillas arrived on a big yellow bus. We stood on the field watching as they poured off that bus—fifteen boys, mostly on the large side, plus some parents and other kids to cheer them on.

"Are those fifth graders?" I asked nobody in particular.

Henry's mouth was hanging open in terror. "They look like eighth graders to me. Maybe ninth."

Pow-Pow had already warned us that we didn't stand a chance against St. Anselm. Now that we saw them in person, we understood. We were silent. Our whole team. Even Webby.

During warm-up the St. Anselm players sped down the field like tigers, even though their mascot is a gorilla. They took pounding shots at the goal, one after another, *boom! boom! boom!* They were so big that when they ran down the field it felt like the earth was shaking. (You probably think I'm exaggerating but I swear I'm not.)

Just before the game began we lined up and the St. Anselm coach led his players past us to shake each of our puny hands with their big beefy ones. I saw the St. A.'s players saying something in a low voice to each of our players, but I couldn't tell what it was. At first I figured they were saying something like "Nice to meet you," or "Let's have a good game." But when the first St. A. player got close to me I could hear what he said to Henry.

"You've got a girl on your team? Maybe you're all girls," Gorilla 1 grunted.

Gorilla 2 snorted, then asked, "What did the Gorilla do to the Turtle?"

At first, I figured he was talking to Henry. But then I realized he was talking to me.

"Is that supposed to be a riddle?" I replied.

Gorilla 2 thought about it for a second, as if the word *riddle* was itself a riddle. Then he nodded his huge head.

"Think about it," he said.

But I didn't need to think about it. I knew what he was getting at.

What does a gorilla do to a turtle?

A gorilla crushes a turtle with one hand.

At this point, the third Gorilla in line spoke up.

"Foyes Island?" he said. "More like *Girls* Island."

"That doesn't make sense," I told him.

"Bwa ha ha!" he replied. "You're going down, Shorty."

And I'm not even that short!

"We'll crush you sissies," Gorilla 2 proclaimed.

"We'll see," Webby, the last person in our line, shot back. "You know what they say—the bigger you are, the harder you fall. And I'm guessing the rocks in your head will make you fall even faster. She may be a girl, but at least she knows how to tie her shoes."

All three Gorillas looked down at their sneakers.

"*And*," Webby added, "she's smart enough not to fall for a stupid your-shoelace-is-untied joke."

For a second, it looked like the Gorillas wanted to peel Webby like a banana. I knew that feeling—but not this time. The other Turtles had been too surprised by the Gorillas' trash talk to say anything back. But not Webby. He's not intimidated by anybody.

What came next, Bess, was the most brutal soccer game I have ever been in or seen. The Gorillas scored two goals in the first ten minutes. Our team was stunned. But then we woke up. My fellow Turtles started passing the ball to me. Maybe they thought the Gorillas were afraid to attack a girl.

They thought wrong.

At first the Gorillas did kind of leave me alone. They probably assumed I wasn't any good, so they didn't guard me.

But then Zach M. passed the ball to Henry, who passed it to me. I took a shot and scored! We were all cheering and jumping up and down, and one of the big Gorillas stuck his foot out under me and tripped me. I collapsed in the dirt. But I didn't let that stop me. I got up and brushed myself off. Resume play.

Now that I'd scored a goal I was fair game. The Gorillas taunted me and jeered at me, calling out, "Girl Turtles! Girl Turtles!" It made them sound like three-year-olds. But somehow it still hurt.

What's wrong with a girl turtle anyway?

The Gorillas took another shot, but Gilbert blocked it. Yes, you heard me right—GILBERT BLOCKED IT. We were all so shocked that Yucky G. had blocked a good shot that it took us a few seconds to recover. He grinned so wide I thought his face would split in two.

Now the Gorillas were MAD. Next time I got the ball, one of them tripped me again. I looked to the ref to call a foul but he didn't see it. Unfair!

Webby started yelling, "Ref! Are you blind? Tripping! Call the foul!"

The ref blew his whistle and threatened to throw Webby out of the game for insulting him. Pow-Pow talked the ref down and Webby stayed in the game. Next time I got the ball, Webby was in perfect position to take a shot, so I passed to him and he scored. Tie game! Webby ran over to me and slapped me five. We were all cheering again, which the Gorillas hated.

Next possession, the Gorillas dribbled downfield. One kicked a high pass, and another one headed it right into my face! I ducked, but the ball grazed the top of my head.

"Hey!" I called out to the offending Gorilla. "You did that on purpose!"

"Get off the field, girl!" he sneered.

"I belong here as much as you!" I yelled back.

"Stop picking on her!" Webby chimed in. "She's the star of our team!"

Really. That's what he said.

The Gorilla laughed, then said, "Is this a girls team or a boys team?"

"It's a soccer team!" Webby answered, getting right in the Gorilla's face.

The refs stepped in before the fight could become a real fight. Webby came over to me.

"Don't listen to them, Claire," he told me. "Keep doing what you're doing. We're going to win this thing."

I was shocked. My feet felt glued to the ground. Then I snapped out of it and ran down the field.

I passed the ball to Henry, but the Gorillas intercepted it. They drove it down the field and took another shot at Gilbert. Missed again. Gilbert threw the ball to Webby. He dribbled all the way down the field until he was blocked by a bunch of Gorillas. He passed the ball to Henry, who passed it back to Webby, even though he was heavily guarded. Webby passed it to me, and I kicked it as hard as I could.

GOOOOAAALLLL!!!!

We jumped and screamed with happiness. We were in the lead! The boys hoisted me on their shoulders and carried me around the field, chanting, "Tur-tles! Tur-tles! Tur-tles!"

Bess, it was a great moment. For once I felt like I really belonged on that team.

The ref blew his whistle. The game wasn't over yet. We had two minutes left to play.

Now the Gorillas were really mad. And they were relentless. They kicked shot after shot at Gilbert. He caught one, caught another . . . then missed one.

Tie game again. Three to three.

Twenty seconds to go. I kicked the ball to Webby, but a Gorilla intercepted it. Webby elbowed him. It might have been an accident, maybe. But the ref didn't think so. He blew his whistle. Foul! The Gorillas got a penalty shot.

We lined up in front of Gilbert to help him block the shot. Gilbert was nervous. I could hear his teeth rattling.

The Gorilla took the shot—and it went in.

The ref blew the whistle. Game over. The Gorillas won.

The weird thing is, I still felt happy. We all did. We slapped each other's hands and said, "Good game."

We didn't win, but we came close. We showed those Gorillas we can play in their league. It was a kind of victory.

I waved to my parents as I ran off the field. Gabe and Jim were there too.

Pow-Pow told us to go to our lockers and change. Everybody on the team went into the boys' locker room except me, of course. I was all alone in the clubhouse.

I could hear them laughing and cheering and towel-snapping and joking around without me. This huge party, taking place in a room that I wasn't allowed to go into.

I felt lonely.

I looked at the drawings on my wall, thinking that if I didn't have that room, at least I had this one. But something was different. I could tell even before I knew what it was.

I scanned the walls until I spotted the change. Someone had sneaked in and drew x's over Starshine's eyes! To make it look like he was dead!!!!

I started to cry, just a little bit. Not flowing tears, but my eyes got wet. I couldn't help it. I was sad and I was mad, and sometimes I cry when I'm mad.

The prowler had struck again.

A Ghostly Shadow

When I got home from school today, I ran straight to the stable to check on Starshine. He was fine, munching on hay. Dad saw how worried I was and asked me what was wrong. I told him what had been done to my picture (although I didn't tell him where the picture was), and he said not to worry about the *x*'s. It had to be a joke, he said. I hope he's right. If anything ever happened to Starshine or Bruno, I would cry so hard my eyes would fall out of my skull.

Tonight, after everybody went to bed, I got up and stared out the window at the water. The moon made it shimmer. It looked pretty, but also spooky. I kept thinking that you can see the very same moon, Bess, all the way out in California. I wondered if you were looking at it too.

A light breeze was blowing, and the trees made shadows on the grass. I thought I saw something move across the yard.

Probably just the moonlight playing tricks on me, I told myself.

But then I saw it again. Something moving. A shadow.

It dashed toward *Swifty*, where she sits near the stable, under her tarp. I thought of poor Starshine, innocently sleeping in the stable, all alone. He sleeps standing up and he snores! He's so sweet. What if the clubhouse prowler was coming to get him?

I slipped downstairs and ran out the back door without stopping to put shoes on. I was wearing my flannel pajamas, the ones with the red stripes. It was chilly out. The ground felt damp and cold on my bare feet. Clouds blew across the moon, making it hard to see.

I ran to the stable but nobody was there. Starshine woke up and nodded at me, like he was asking, *What are you doing here at this hour?*

I almost saddled him up to go for a ride, just because. I've never ridden him at night. It's probably dangerous. He could trip or fall into a hole or something, and hurt his foot. Plus, my parents would kill me.

I double-checked the stable and circled all around it. No one was there. So where did the shadowy figure go?

Maybe it was a fox, or a coyote. Maybe there hadn't been a shadowy figure at all. I was beginning to think I'd imagined it. The moon and the clouds can play tricks on your eyes.

I started back to the house. I remembered how I'd found Bruno hiding in *Swifty* a while back. I looked at the boat. The silhouette of the tarp looked kind of lumpy in the moonlight.

Maybe Bruno was hiding in there again.

I crept up to the boat, silent as a fox. The tarp didn't move.

One, two, three—I ripped the tarp off the boat!

Empty. The lump had been made by a couple of life jackets I'd tossed under the tarp. I felt under the bow, just to make sure nobody was hiding there.

Then I heard a *clunk* coming from the boat shed. Or did I?

Maybe it was a ghost! I have ghosts on my mind a lot lately, because of the holiday play.

Maybe it was the ghost of Smuggler Joe.

I stopped to listen. The water lapped at the shore—it sounded a lot like Bruno lapping at his water dish. A breeze rustled the last leaves left on the trees. A gull called out from a nest on the buoy past our dock. I stayed very still. I heard all those night sounds, but the shed stayed quiet.

I walked over there, just to be sure. The cold dirt squished between my toes. I shivered and wished I'd thrown on my rain boots.

If someone's in the shed, I thought, *I probably shouldn't go in there. I should run back to the house and tell Mom and Dad.*

My feet were so cold I was hopping up and down on my toes. Ghost or no ghost, he must be freezing too. I remembered what Mom had said about offering him iced tea. How he'd never hurt an Islander.

I whispered, "Come sleep in our house! It's warm!"

I thought about it a second and added: "But not in my room. I'm too scared of you!"

Then I hurried back into the house before my parents could figure out I was gone.

I tiptoed up the stairs. All was quiet. Everyone was sleeping.

I got into bed, but I was kind of shaken up. I couldn't fall asleep. So I decided to write and tell you what happened.

I'm still looking out the window. Maybe Smuggler Joe is out there in the shed right now!

Do ghosts get cold?

I think I'll take some food out to the shed, and a blanket, and leave them there for him. Just in case.

Still alive,
Your friend Claire

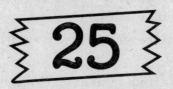

25

The Food Is Gone

Dear Bess,

This morning when I got up for school, I threw my coat over my pajamas, stepped into my boots, and hurried out to see if anyone had been in the shed last night.

The blanket I'd left for Joe was there. But the food was gone!

A raccoon could have eaten it, I guess. But I like to think Joe had a nice supper.

I walked back to the house, shaking my head. What's wrong with me? Leaving food out for a ghost?

A person who does that must be pretty lonely.

Bess, I miss you so much. I also miss Henry.

Why won't he be friends with me anymore?

I don't understand it. I was a girl before. And we were friends. I'm still a girl, but now he doesn't want to be friends. The only thing that changed is that you moved away.

And that Henry became friends with Webby.

26

Humbug

The play is not going well. Gilbert can never remember his lines, and Webby plays Marley's Ghost with a big booming voice and stiff arms and legs like a zombie, or maybe Optimus Prime. Mr. Harper keeps telling him to tone it down, but he won't.

The dress rehearsal is tomorrow afternoon. We had a costume fitting today. My costumes are all frilly dresses and dumb bonnets. Even my Ghost robe comes with a white nightcap.

Mr. Harper asked us to come in tonight for an extra rehearsal. He seems very nervous. I don't want the play to be bad, but I'm more focused on Operation Make Henry Be My Friend Again. Now is the time. Tonight I will put my plan into action.

Wish me luck (since no one else will),
Claire

27

Operation Make Henry Be
My Friend Again

Dear Bess,

I'm home from rehearsal. It's late, and I'm supposed to be in bed. But I can't sleep.

I put Operation Make Henry Be My Friend Again into action tonight. Perhaps you are wondering what my great plan was. Here's what happened.

Rehearsal was mostly over. Mr. H. let everybody go home except for me and Henry and Cal, who plays Young Scrooge. Mr. H. wanted us to practice the Ghost of Christmas Past scenes, because I have so many tricky character/costume changes. He focused on the part where I'm Young Scrooge's girlfriend, Belle, and I tell him the engagement is off because he's too greedy. Mr. H. said he wanted tears to spring to his eyes when he watched that scene, and right now all he gets is indigestion.

We practiced it until tears came to Mr. H.'s eyes. He said the tears were not from sentiment or sadness but from being tired and frustrated, but technically they were tears, so he kept his word and let us go.

It was after eight at night. Cal went home. The whole school was dark, except for the stage, where we were rehearsing, and the rooms backstage where we change into our costumes.

Henry has a little closet to himself to change in, since he's the star. I was still wearing my Ghost of Christmas Past costume. I was headed for Henry's changing room, ready to scare the daylights out of him, when I got a glimpse of myself in the mirror.

I didn't look the least bit scary. The Ghost of Christmas Past is not a scary ghost.

I decided to borrow Webby's Ghost of Christmas Future costume. Christmas Future is terrifying. It's all about death, and the costume is basically just a big black robe with a hood, so it fits anybody. I threw it on over my Christmas Past costume. Then I got my laptop and hid it under the robe.

Henry's dressing room door was ajar. I saw a beam of light spill out from the room into the dark hall. I peeked in. He was still in his costume, wiping off his old man makeup.

I pulled the hood low over my face and moaned like a ghost. Henry didn't look up. Didn't pause. Just kept wiping makeup off his forehead with a paper towel.

"Heeennnnrrryyyy . . ." I moaned. "Oooooooh."

Now he looked up. He saw me in the robe, my face hidden by the hood, and looked scared for a second. Then he said, "Webby, what are you doing here?"

I stepped into the little room. "I'm not Webby," I said

94

in a ghostly whisper. "I'm the Ghost of School Years Past. *Your* past."

"Quit it, Webby."

I pulled my computer from the folds of the robe and opened it. "Henry Long. You have been a baaaaad friend. You used to be a goooood friend. Let me show you scenes from your past, when you used to have a heart."

"Oh, it's you, Claire," Henry said heartlessly.

I'd made a slide show of pictures of you, me, and Henry—pictures of fun times we've had over the years. Our birthday parties. Me and him sitting at the edge of the town pool with our feet in the water, splashing the other kids. Me and him sailing together. That one Halloween when the three of us dressed up as the Three Blind Mice. Me and Henry on the dock with our arms around each other's shoulders and our life jackets on. And every year for the past four years, the picture my mother took of us on the first day of school. Me and Henry with our new lunchboxes, standing on my front steps in first grade, second grade, third grade, fourth grade . . .

But not fifth grade. Not this year. Because this year Henry didn't show up.

"We walked to school together every day," I said in my ghost voice. "For all those years. Until now. Why did it stop, Henry? Why?"

It was a great slide show, Bess. You would have gotten choked up. And I think it was working on Henry. I couldn't tell for sure, but I saw him swallow hard a couple of times.

"You see, Henry," I said, still talking spookily, "we've had a wonderful life together. A lifelong friendship. You wouldn't want to throw that away, would you?"

It was working, Bess. I swear it was. His eyes were wet, or at least wettish. He opened his mouth and was about to say something. But then there was a crash from the stage.

"Pay no atteeeennntion to that," I said to Henry. I wanted to keep his attention on our friendship. "It's prooobbbably just Mr. Haaaarrperrrr."

"Cut the ghost voice, Claire," Henry snapped.

He stood up and walked slowly out of his dressing room, down the hall, to the wings of the stage. I followed him reluctantly.

The stage was dark.

"See, it's nothing," I whispered.

Henry reached for the stage lights and flipped them on.

A rope lay tangled in the middle of the stage. It hadn't been there before. It seemed like it had fallen from the sky.

We looked up. Another rope dangled from the rafters.

"It must have fallen somehow," I said.

"Yeah," Henry said. "But how?"

I guess Henry was spooked by my ghost show because he stared up into the dark and shouted, "Who's up there?"

No one answered.

I wanted to say, "It's Smuggler Joe," but I bit my tongue.

Mr. Harper walked out of the wings. "I thought I turned these lights off." He reached for the switch and flicked the stage lights off. "Let's clear the premises, kids. Time to go home."

"In a minute," I said. My slide show had an amazing finish and Henry hadn't seen it yet.

"No, now," Mr. Harper said. "It's late." Then he peered at my face under the Ghost of Christmas Future hood. "Claire? What are you doing in Webby's costume?"

"Nothing—"

"Put it away right now and let's get out of here. Mr. Jones wants to lock up the building."

I looked at Henry, but he wouldn't meet my eye. The opportunity was lost.

I put the robe away and the three of us left together. Henry's dad was waiting to drive him home, and my dad was waiting to walk me home.

"See you in the morning, kids," Mr. Harper said as he got into his car.

"Bye, Henry," I called.

"Bye," he said.

Dad and I started walking home. It was cold out. I wished he'd picked me up in the truck.

"How was rehearsal?" he asked.

"I don't know," I said. "I'll find out tomorrow."

"Why is that?" He sounded puzzled, but I didn't feel like explaining.

I'll explain to you, though, Bess, even though I know you already understand.

When we got home, I went to my room and watched the end of the slide show, the part Henry didn't get to see. There's a picture from last summer, me and Henry sharing the big box of saltwater taffy he brought back for me from Ocean City. We each took a long striped piece and plastered it over our front teeth, so it looked like we had taffy braces. He thought that was so funny.

The last shot shows me and him at age three, sitting in a baby pool in his backyard. We're both wearing swim diapers and he's got his little baby head on my little baby shoulder. It's a real heart tugger.

If only he'd had a chance to see it.

Tomorrow morning I will wait to see if my Ghost of Henrys Past slide show softened Henry's heart at all. I will wait to see if he stops by my house to pick me up.

Good night, Bess.
Claire

Who Needs Boys?

Dear Bess,

It was bright and sunny and cold this morning. I bundled up in my winter coat and sat on the front porch, waiting to see if Henry would stop to pick me up. To see if the old pictures of us had had any effect on his frozen heart.

Gabe said he'd wait ten minutes—inside, not out on the porch—and then he was walking to school without me. Mom said she didn't want Gabe walking to school by himself and she didn't want either one of us to be late, so I had to leave with Gabe in ten minutes.

I sat on the steps, watching my breath puff out of my mouth like frosty smoke. I studied the road for something moving on the horizon, a black dot in the distance, any sign that someone was coming. A truck roared past with a load of fish in the back. A car drove by and didn't stop. Mom came out of the house with Gabe, handed me my lunch, and said, "Get going."

I kept glancing over my shoulder as we walked to school, expecting to see Henry running after us to catch up. I felt sure my Ghost of Christmas Past slide show would remind him how much fun we used to have. I hoped it would change his mind about me, about being friends. *I should have waited five more minutes*, I said to myself. *Five more minutes and he would have come.* I just couldn't believe my plan hadn't worked.

Henry was already at school when I got there, telling Webby how a rope fell from above the stage last night, all by itself.

"Nobody was there," Henry was saying. "It had to be a ghost."

"It could have been an accident," Webby said. He didn't sound spooked at all.

"It was Smuggler Joe!" Henry swore. "Claire said— I mean, I'm pretty sure it was. Who else could it have been?"

He wouldn't even admit that he'd been with me!

My plan was a total failure.

He's got a heart of stone.

What changed him, Bess? I think I know.

Henry's change of heart is the fault of one person: Webster Peterson.

Webby stole Henry! He convinced him not to be friends with me anymore.

I should give up on Henry. I'll live without friends. It's okay. I've got food, water, shelter, all that stuff. Parents. I've got brothers, even if they're worse than useless. I've got Bruno and Starshine. Animals. I'll be friends with the animals. Who needs people? Not me. I don't need people, especially not BOY people.

Your friendless friend,
Claire

P.S. I'll get that Webby if it's the last thing I do.
P.P.S. Time for a new plan.

29

Opening Night

Tonight was the opening night of the play. Here is the Foyes Island *Foghorn*'s review:

Henry Long stars as Scrooge in the Foyes Island Elementary School Production of
A Christmas Carol
By Edward Strickland, Foghorn Theater Critic and FIES Art Teacher

Fifth grader Henry Long made his stage debut last night in Foyes Island Elementary School's all-male production of A Christmas Carol. *Correction: almost all-male. The show featured one actress, fifth grader Claire Warren, as the Ghost of Christmas Past, Fan, Belle, Mrs. Fezziwig, Mrs. Cratchit, Fred's Wife, and Scrooge's Housekeeper. She did an admirable job of changing costumes in record time, though she did forget to remove Belle's bonnet before reverting back to playing the Ghost.*

A minor quibble about what was, overall, a very fine show.

As Scrooge, Henry Long showed his range from grouchy and mean to happy and generous. Webster Peterson was a standout as two terrifying Ghosts, Marley and Christmas Future. When he pointed his bony skeleton finger at Scrooge's tombstone, silently menacing in his death-dark hood, he made the audience shiver with cold fear of the grave.

There were a few moments that struck this reviewer as odd choices made by the director, Matthew Harper. For instance, when Marley's Ghost appeared to Scrooge, dragging long, heavy chains behind him, chains representing the sins Marley had committed when he was alive, Claire Warren, as the Housekeeper, trembled appropriately, but then yanked on the chain several times until Marley tripped and fell on his knees, yelping in pain. The Housekeeper then said, in what I assume were ad-libbed lines, "How can your knees hurt if you're a ghost? Huh? Huh?"

The audience laughed, which spoiled the spooky mood of the scene. Still, it must be said, Miss Warren's cockney accent

*was not bad for a girl who has never been
to England.*

It's not like I planned it, Bess. It just happened. I guess
that's called an *ad-lib*.

But back to the review.

Another deviation from the original play came during Act III, when the Ghost of Christmas Future, again played by Mr. Peterson, was showing Scrooge the heartbreak at the Cratchit home caused by the death of Tiny Tim. As the Cratchit family sobbed over the empty hearth and Tiny Tim's useless crutch, the Ghost of the Future suddenly began to twitch. At first it was hardly noticeable, but after a moment it became clear that the Ghost was scratching himself very enthusiastically. He was soon wriggling and squirming in his long black robe, scratching as if bugs were crawling on him. It was an unconventional way of showing the Ghost's own bad feelings about the sad scenes he was showing to Scrooge. At least, that's how this critic understood the actor's choice.

Most of the cast seemed taken aback by this behavior but stayed in their roles. However, Mrs. Cratchit (played, as noted, by Claire Warren) did not seem a bit surprised and could not stop laughing, breaking character. In fairness, she may have broken character on purpose, as a way of showing the broken heart of a mother who has lost her child, and the madness caused by that heartbreak.

This critic has seen many productions of A Christmas Carol *in his fifteen years at the* Foghorn—FIES *seems to do it about every other year—but he's never seen one like this. If you're looking for a fresh, experimental take on a holiday classic, give this year's* Christmas Carol *a spin.*

3 Stars★★★

Mr. Strickland gave us 3 out of 5 stars! Not bad.

Yes, I put itching powder in Webby's Ghost costume. That was not an ad-lib.

Yes, Mr. Harper figured out that I did it.

(I probably shouldn't have laughed so much. But it was just. So. Funny.)

Yes, I got in trouble for it. Mr. H. wanted to fire me from the play, but they couldn't replace me at the last moment because

(1) nobody else knows my lines

(2) there are no other girls to play the girl parts

(3) all the boys would probably refuse to dress up as women to play the girl parts.

The play will run the rest of this weekend. As punishment, Mr. H. gave me detention every afternoon until

Christmas break and is making me write an essay about The Dangers of Pranking.

It doesn't matter. At the end of the play, as the curtain went down, the audience was on their feet clapping and cheering. Sure, they were parents cheering for their own kids, and they would have stood and clapped if we'd sung "Mary Had a Little Lamb" fifty times in a row, out of tune. But it felt good.

Your friend,
Claire the Dangerous Prankster

Part 3

Dance of the Squares

April

Bowling

Dear Bess,

It's that time of year again. Spring.
With spring comes—

(1) my birthday
(2) the Square Dance

But not in that order.

Remember that guy they hired to call the square
dance last year, Hee Haw Higgins? He kept saying,
"Gents, bow to your partner! Ladies, curtsy to the gents!"
and made half the boys do curtsies?

Sure you do. People don't forget traumatic experi-
ences like that.

He's coming back. Two weeks from today.

Yes, it's Foyes Island Elementary's Famous Spring
Square Dance. Attendance required.

Mr. Unitas announced the return of the dance today
at Assembly as if he expected everybody to jump up and
down and cheer. Instead: groans. He would have gotten

more cheers if he'd announced that we were getting all our teeth pulled out—attendance required.

Mr. Unitas loves his traditions. When he heard the groans, he said, "Aw, come on now! Foyes Island El has had a square dance every spring since 1967! We had it when I was a student"—back in the last century—"and, doggonit, we're going to have it this year—whether you all like it or not."

More groans.

"Don't you understand?" He wouldn't let it go. "If we stop one of our great traditions now, we'll never start it up again. And then it will be dead! Gone! No more square dance. Forever!"

THAT made everyone cheer. RIP Spring Square Dance! Let's put it out of its misery.

"Now, boys," Mr. Unitas said, "and Claire . . ."

That's how he always addresses us now, as "Boys . . . and Claire."

"I know we've only got one girl in the school this year, so you're all going to have to dance with each other. But that's okay in square dancing! It's more about hopping around than anything else. It's practically a sport. Why, when I was a pup, they used to teach square dancing in gym."

Nobody was convinced.

This is terrible.

But . . . maybe not *that* terrible. Because I have an idea. I could use the square dance to make things better between me and Henry.

Yes, I know, I know, Henry again. I gave up on him. That's what I said. I decided to live a life without friends.

But Bess, a life without friends is very hard.

Maybe you don't remember what winters are like here in the East, now that you live out there in Weather Heaven. They're cold. The wind blows off the water, and it's no fun to ride Starshine or walk through the woods with Bruno. Dad and the other watermen still go out fishing and oystering, of course, but it's too cold for sailing.

This past winter, the inlet nearly froze over. I went skating on Perry Pond with Gabe and Jim a few times. I read a lot of books. Other than that, winter was three whole months of bored and lonely.

A few of my classmates had bowling parties, but they didn't invite me. One Saturday I took Gabe to Bay Lanes. It happened to be Zach M.'s birthday party.

I'm not saying I didn't know that before we went. Maybe I did and maybe I didn't. It's a free country, and Gabe and I have as much right to go bowling as anybody else, birthday or no birthday.

We got a lane right next to the party and bowled all afternoon, just me and Gabe. I got a few strikes too. I creamed Gabe. He kept getting gutter balls and was close to tears most of the time.

First graders. They're not good for much.

My point is: I was standing right next to Zach and Henry and Webby and those guys for *three hours*, and they didn't even say hello. Gilbert would have, if he'd been there, but he hadn't been invited either. The boys acted like they didn't see me. They were whooping and hollering and slapping each other's hands as if it were the Super Bowl.

I tried to catch Henry's eye. Once, after I bowled a strike, I jumped up and down like the boys were doing, and slapped Gabe's hand and shouted, "All right! Yeah!" At first Gabe got excited too but pretty soon he figured out it was all pretend, and when I raised my hand to slap his again, he pretended he didn't notice.

I glanced over at Henry to see if he was admiring my great bowling skills. But he never seemed to be facing in my direction. It was like he refused to turn his head to the left, which wasn't easy since it meant he couldn't look at half the bowling alley.

That's what it's been like all winter, Bess. I don't understand what Henry's problem is. I've decided to call a truce. I surrender. I'm going to make a peace gesture.

My peace gesture will be: to ask Henry to the square dance. I figure, since everyone in the school has to go, and there is only one girl for the boys to dance with— me—all the boys will want to go with me. I'm expecting a lot of boys to ask me to go with them. Being with me at the dance will be like a status symbol. I can grant this status upon any boy I choose, like a genie granting wishes or a queen touching a boy's shoulder with a sword and making him a knight.

That's what I'm thinking.

I hope Henry will appreciate my peace gesture. I further hope that we will have a good time acting goofy at the dance, and from then on we will be friends again.

Your bowling queen,
Claire

31

The Bathroom Prowler Strikes Again

Hi Bess,

I'm writing to you from the clubhouse. Someone has vandalized my wall once again!

Somebody broke in here and drew a picture of me at the bowling alley. It shows me with my arm out, having just thrown the ball, which is in the gutter. There's a speech balloon over my head saying, "Missed again!"

It's not true! I got three strikes! I'm a good bowler! I'm very upset.

Whoever is drawing on my wall had to be at the bowling alley on the day of Zach M.'s birthday party. That leaves five suspects: Zach M., Henry, Webby, Cal, and Kevin.

My money is still on Webby.

I made a big X through the drawing. I'll paint over it later. In the meantime, I added some new drawings of my own. It's *my* wall and it should have *my* pictures on it.

Spring is here. A hopeful time. I drew my favorite willow tree, the big one by the water in our backyard. It's starting to get green. And the dogwood in the front yard will bloom soon, I think. I drew the tree as it is now, with little green buds sticking off the branches.

As soon as I leave the clubhouse, I'm going to find Henry and ask him to the dance. I'm tired of fighting. I want peace.

32

I Ask Henry to the Square Dance

I did it. I made my peace gesture.

I found Henry at lunchtime, leaving the cafeteria with Webby.

"Henry," I said, making my voice sound like we talk *all the time*, "can I talk to you for a minute?"

He looked surprised. And before he could answer, Webby said, "See ya," and grinned obnoxiously.

Now Henry looked uncomfortable.

"What do you want?" he asked.

Not a very encouraging start.

I cleared my throat. I felt like I was stepping off a cliff. *Be brave*, I told myself. *You've got nothing to lose.*

"Henry, you know how the square dance is coming up? It's lame, I know, but we have to go, right? So I was wondering if you would like to go with me. We can laugh and make fun of it together, like we did with Bess last year."

A little knot of boys clustered at the end of the hall, watching us. Henry's eyes darted toward them. He shifted his weight from one foot to the other and back again. He looked at the floor, looked at the wall, looked at the ceiling . . . everywhere but at me.

"Sorry, Claire," he said. "I'm not going with anybody."

I couldn't quite believe it.

"So you're saying no?" I asked.

He didn't answer.

I went on. "You have to be there, one way or another. Attendance required. Why not be there with me? Your old friend Claire?"

He looked sort of horrified that I wouldn't drop it. He shook his head and said, "I've got to go."

Then he ran off.

It's funny. I didn't really expect him to say yes. I braced myself for the worst. I told myself he'd probably say no.

But actually hearing it . . . it hurt. It hurt bad.

I went to the clubhouse to recover. I was glad I had a place to go where no one could see me.

Then I drew a scene on my wall. I drew a little me talking to a little Henry, with a speech bubble coming out of his mouth. I wrote "NO" inside the bubble. I drew a tiny tear on my face.

I guess I could ask another boy, but why bother?

No matter what I do, I'm going to be the round peg at the square dance. Har har.

33

How to Get Revenge on Webby

I came up with a prank to play on Webby. What do you think of this?

We all go to the dance. Mr. Unitas and Pow-Pow are making us choose partners and line up in two rows, while Hee Haw Higgins talks through the mike, saying stuff like, "Yee haw, this is a real country hoedown! Yahoo!" and whatever. All the boys will be dragging their feet, grumbling about how they don't feel like dancing.

Meanwhile, I've got Dad's old boat horn, the one that makes that funny sound? I hide the horn under my jacket or something. And every time Webby bows to his partner, I honk the horn. Everyone will laugh at him! And when they find out I'm the one playing the joke, I'll be their hero.

The dance is this weekend. Maybe I should keep thinking.

And, in case you forgot (but I know you would never forget), my birthday is the weekend after that. I usually look forward to my birthday. Remember last year, on my tenth birthday, when my dad took you, me, and Henry to the Spring Carnival in St. Anselm? And we rode all the rides and ate ice cream and Dad got a bunch of carnies dressed as zombies to sing "Happy Birthday" to me in the haunted house? Even the guy getting sliced open on the buzz saw table was into it.

I'll never top that. I'm not expecting to. But I don't know if I should even try to have a birthday party this year. Who would come?

Mom is insisting, though. She said I'm having a party if it kills her. She's going to make a big cake and she told me to invite everyone in my class. I told her nobody will come but she said, "How will you know for sure if you don't try?"

She doesn't get it. I don't WANT to know for sure that nobody wants to come to my birthday party.

Party Invitation

Thanks to Mom, who would not stop bugging me, I sent out seven invitations, one to every boy in my class. Here's one for you, Bess. If only you could come! The two of us would have a great time. If you came, I wouldn't wish for anything else.

YOU'RE INVITED to:
Claire's Eleventh Birthday Party
At her house
303 Eliot Point Road
Saturday, April 23
Two o'clock
Games, cake, piñata, the usual . . .
If you can't make it, don't worry, you won't
miss anything.
RSVP

I haven't heard back from anyone yet.

How much are plane tickets from California?
Claire

Party Invitation Part Two

Dear Bess,

What do you mean, it's not a very inviting invitation? I INVITED people. I asked them to come. That's the definition of *inviting*.

Okay, I know what you mean. Mom said the same thing.

"You have to make the party sound like fun if you want people to come," she told me. "You can't tell them they won't be missing anything!"

But I sent the invitations anyway.

Maybe I'M the one who wouldn't be missing anything if nobody came. What am I going to do at an all-boys party? Kickbox? Pop the balloons and smash the cake? If anyone in the world knows what boys do, it's me. All they can talk about is smells and snot and sports. Oh, and video games. Not that there's anything wrong with video games. But I think they're really, really boring to talk about.

I hear you saying I'm not being fair. Not all the boys are thugs or gross all the time. Most of them aren't.

Webby definitely is. Yes, he was nice to me one afternoon during a soccer game. But after that: nothing.

Which didn't stop my mom from forcing me to send him an invitation.

Really, forget about visiting from California.

I think I'm going to move there instead.

Claire

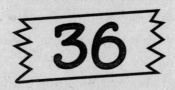

Party Invitation Part Three

Dear Bess,

I sent out the invitations four days ago. My classmates have definitely received them. But no one has said a word to me about the party.

This morning at school, Mr. Harper was teaching us about verbs in language arts. He told us about infinitives—to be, to eat, to go, etc., and showed us how to conjugate them:

<u>To Be</u>
I am
You are
He, she, it is
We are
You are
They are

After a few rounds of this he asked, "Who can give us another verb to conjugate?"
I raised my hand.

"To invite," I said after he called on me. "I invite, you invite, he invites, we invite, you invite, they invite."

"Good," Mr. Harper said. "Who has another one?"

I didn't wait for him to call on me this time. I said, "To reply. I reply. YOU reply. Or maybe you *don't* reply?"

I gave all the boys in the class my most intense stink eye. They shrank back in their seats. (As you know, I give good stink eye.) But not one of them said anything.

Mr. Harper looked mystified.

"You didn't finish conjugating that verb, Claire," he pointed out. "But I think you've got the idea."

The bell rang and everybody went to lunch. I was going to take my lunch to the clubhouse to eat alone as usual, but Mr. Harper stopped me and said he wanted to talk to me.

"Is anything bothering you, Claire?" he asked.

"No," I answered.

"Really? Because you don't seem very happy. Last year you were a lot more cheerful."

"I was?"

Hearing him say it made me sad. Sadder than I was already feeling. It's just that I didn't see any point in telling him my troubles, because what could he do about them? Could he bring you back from California? Could he magically make a new girl appear in town?

He went on. "I know it's hard, being the only girl in the whole school. Do the boys pick on you?"

I couldn't really look him in the eye. "Most of them are okay."

"Is one of them bothering you?"

Yes, I thought. *Webby. And Henry.*

But if I told him, he would then go tell them I said they were bothering me. And I didn't want them to know they were bothering me. I wanted them to think that nothing they did had any effect on me. That I was completely free of them. That they had no power over me at all.

So I said, "No. Everyone is very nice to me."

I think he knew I was lying, but he didn't press me.

"Okay. Just know you can come talk to me any time you like. Got it?"

"Got it."

Outside in the hall, there were shouts and laughter. Mr. Harper and I went to the door. Mr. Jones had just mopped the floor and Gilbert had slipped on the wet spot and fallen. Webby was pointing at him and screaming with laughter, just like he did to me on the soccer field.

"What a jerk," I said under my breath . . . but not that far under my breath, because Mr. Harper heard me.

"Mm-hmm" was all he said back.

Mm-hmm,
Claire

The Square Dance

Dear Bess,

Tonight was the square dance.

Today at Assembly Mr. Unitas reminded us that we all had to go. He said, for the tenth time, "Attendance is required."

Maybe he knew something I didn't.

I put on some blue jeans and a red-and-white-checked shirt that I thought looked "country." I ate an early dinner and said a grim good-bye to my brothers and mother. Dad drove me to school. He escorted me to the door of the gym. It was all lit up and we could hear fiddle music playing. It sure looked like a dance was happening there.

Dad kissed me good-bye. "I'll pick you up in a couple of hours," he said. Then he drove home.

I walked into the gym. Hee Haw Higgins stood on a platform with a microphone, dancing in a circle around a fiddle player. The teachers huddled by the refreshments table. They looked strangely relaxed, teasing each other and laughing and joking.

I've seen the teachers act that way before, just once.

Last year, I happened to walk by the teachers' lounge when the door was open. I peeked inside. Mr. Strickland was telling some kind of funny story, and all other teachers were sipping their coffee and hanging on his every word, and when he said, "I left my harp in Sam Clam's disco," they all broke up laughing. Not in a classroom joke way, but the way my parents laugh when they have friends over for dinner and think we've gone to bed and don't know we're spying on them.

That's what the teachers looked like when I got to the square dance tonight. But when they noticed me, they stiffened up.

"Hey!" Mr. Harper walked over to greet me. "One of you showed!"

"What?" I asked.

I looked around. The gym did feel very empty.

That's because it *was* empty. I was the only student there.

None of the boys had shown up.

"Claire!" Mr. Unitas shouted. "I'm glad you could make it." The teachers all cracked up again. They were still a little bit in their no-kids-are-around mode.

Hee Haw clapped his hands. "Come on, everybody! Let's start the hoedown!" Behind him was a little band, a trio—a fiddle player, a stand-up bass, and a guitar, all wearing cowboy hats and cowboy boots. Hee Haw gave the signal and they started playing.

"Line up, everybody!" he called. "Ladies on the left, gents on the right."

Ms. Ruiz, Ms. Teitelman, Mrs. Grimes, and I were the only ladies there. We lined up, and the men lined up across from us. We were outnumbered ten to four, so a few of the men joined our side. Hee Haw and Mr. Unitas were not going to let us get away with not dancing, not with the band there and all. So we shrugged our shoulders and started dancing. Hee Haw told us what to do, just like last year.

"Gents, bow to your partner," he called. The men stepped forward and bowed.

"Ladies, curtsy to the gents." My line stepped forward and curtsied. The men in our line bowed, except for Mr. Strickland, who got a big laugh by curtsying and batting his eyes at Mr. Unitas.

Then Hee Haw did his thing. See if you can imagine the dance from the calls he made:

> Swing your partner round and round, till the
> hole in your head makes a whistling sound,
> Ace of Diamonds, Jack of Spades, meet your
> partner and promenade!
> Swing with Mary, swing with Grace,
> Allemande left with Old Prune Face!
> Stop where you are and don't be blue,
> The music quit, so I will too.

After a few rounds of dancing we stopped to take a breather. It's real exercise, square dancing. I went to the refreshments table for a soda. Suddenly, the gym door banged open and there stood Gilbert, all out of breath like us.

"Sorry I'm late!" he called out.

I've never seen Mr. Unitas so happy to see a student before.

"Gilbert!" he called back. "Join the fun!"

Gilbert came over to me.

"Can I be your partner?" he asked.

I had been dancing with Mr. Harper, but he stepped aside.

"Um, okay," I said.

I mean, Gilbert was the only person in the room close to my height, so it made sense.

Before we started dancing, I noticed he had a toy handcuff attached to one of his wrists.

"What's that for?" I asked him.

Gilbert tugged at the handcuff. "I can't get it off. Webby and those guys tried to keep me from coming, so they handcuffed me to my kitchen table. I managed to get one hand free, but this cuff won't open."

"Where are the other guys?"

"Boycotting the dance. Not just in our grade, but in every grade. They wanted me to stay home, but I wouldn't. They had to handcuff me to the table to stop me from coming, Claire."

I tried to think of something to say, something that showed I appreciated the gesture but didn't want to encourage him to like me any more than he already did.

What I ended up with was, "You're very . . . persistent."

Now that I think of it, maybe Gilbert deserved better than that.

"I knew you'd be here all by yourself," he said. "And, well, I wanted to dance with you."

At that point, Mr. Harper stepped in and said, "Let me help you get that off."

He found a screwdriver and removed the handcuff from Gilbert's wrist.

"Now you won't bonk us with it when we're swinging you around," Mr. Harper said.

Everybody had a cool drink. Then the band started playing again, and we lined up to dance.

Hee Haw called out:

It ain't going to rain, it ain't going to snow, all
join hands and away we go!
Swing your partner round and round, any old
way but upside down.
Swing her, Mack, don't break her back!

Gilbert is a very enthusiastic dancer. He swung me around so hard I twirled off and bumped into Ms. Teitelman! But she didn't mind. We were all laughing and dancing and swinging each other by the elbow and stumbling around getting dizzy. It was kind of fun, actually. Webby and those guys missed a pretty good time.

Dad got to the gym a little early to pick me up. Mr. Unitas waved to him. "Hey, John! Join the party."

I looked at Gilbert. "Oh no," I said under my breath. I didn't want my dad dancing!

But Gilbert said, "What difference does it make? It's just us and the teachers anyway."

He was right. I shrugged and we all did one more Virginia reel. Dad really got into it, just like I knew he would.

*First you whistle, then you sing. All join hands
and make a ring.
Do-si-do, don't you know, you can't catch a
rabbit till it starts to snow.
Right and left on heel and toe, peek behind
you, look there's Joe!
Comb your hair and tie your shoe, promenade
home like you always do.
Ladies to their seats and gents all foller, thank
the fiddler and kiss the caller.*

We all bowed to the band and clapped for them. The dance was over.

I said good night to Gilbert and Mr. Harper and all the other teachers. Then Dad and I got into the car.

"That was fun, wasn't it?" he said.

"Yeah," I admitted.

It was better than I expected, anyway.

"Took me back to my own school days. We had a square dance every spring back then too. Only, more kids showed up . . ."

Dad pulled into the driveway. As the headlights swept across the yard, I thought I saw somebody peek out the shed window. But maybe it was just a reflection in the glass.

A line from one of Hee Haw's calls echoed in my mind: *Peek behind you, look there's Joe!*

I bet he meant Smuggler Joe.

Maybe Hee Haw's calls hid coded messages from the old smuggler days! Some of them *were* kind of hard to understand. Like, what did he mean when he said, *You can't catch a rabbit till it starts to snow?*

Why can't you?

And who's Old Prune Face?

Of course, once Smuggler Joe was in my mind, I couldn't stop thinking about him—and about the face I thought I saw in the shed.

I waited until everybody was asleep, and then I grabbed a flashlight and sneaked outside to look. The shed was empty.

But something glinted on the floor, catching a beam from my flashlight—a glint of light near my right foot. I reached down and picked it up.

It was a gold coin! With a picture of a treasure chest stamped on the front, and some blurry words on the back.

I swept the light over the shed one last time. No one was in there. I put the coin in my pocket and went back inside the house.

I'm looking at it now. It's definitely metal, but I'm not sure it's gold. It's kind of light for gold.

I'll show it to Mom and Dad in the morning and see what they think.

A Doubloon?

At breakfast this morning I showed everyone the coin I'd found in the boat shed.

"Is that a chocolate coin?" Gabe asked.

"No," I told him. "It's metal. I found it in the boat shed last night."

Dad didn't like the sound of that. "What were you doing in the boat shed last night?" he asked.

I didn't want to say I thought I'd seen a face in the window. He would have gotten mad at me for going out there alone.

"I went out there to get . . . my homework. I left it on the worktable."

I don't think Dad believed me, but he let it slide.

Mom picked up the coin and studied it.

"It's not old," she said. "I think it's made of aluminum."

"Let me see," Jim said.

He looked at it. Then he bit it.

"It's a token from the game arcade in St. Anselm," he announced.

"It is?" I asked.

I was hoping it was pirate treasure or smuggler's gold.

Jim nodded. "Yep. See? It says Andy's Arcade."

I should have noticed that before. I had seen letters stamped onto the coin, but I assumed they said something like *Ye Olde Englande*.

"Somebody must have dropped it," Dad said.

I asked Gabe if it was him. He said no. Then I asked Jim and he said, "Not mine. Must belong to one of your friends."

And that was the end of that, as far as they were concerned. But I was still a little mystified. Whoever dropped that token couldn't have been one of my friends, since I don't have any friends.

What do you think, Bess?
Claire

39

Who Keeps Breaking into My Clubhouse?

I didn't do much else the rest of the weekend. I had some social studies homework. I went to the hardware store with Dad to get a winch for the boat. Mom took me to St. Anselm to buy a new pair of rain boots, since my feet grew out of my old ones and it never stops raining.

I took Bruno for a long walk on Saturday and took a cloudy ride on Starshine when the rain stopped. I stared out the window for a while on Saturday night, hoping to catch a glimpse of the shadowy person I thought I'd seen in the boat shed window. But I didn't see anything.

This morning I walked into the clubhouse to find . . . more graffiti! Someone drew on my wall again. And this time I really don't get it.

Here's what the prowler drew: a picture of me (I could tell it was me by my red-checked shirt) at the square dance, dancing with Yucky Gilbert! You can see all the other people who were there too—even my dad.

Webby wasn't there. So how could he know who WAS there? How could he know that Gilbert showed up, or that my dad decided to dance too?

The creepiest thing of all is the speech bubble drawn over Hee Haw Higgins's head. It says, "Peek behind you. Look, there's Joe!"

Which is something that Hee Haw actually said that night.

How could Webby know about that if he wasn't there?

Maybe someone else drew this drawing, someone who is not Webby. I compared the styles of the new picture to the old ones. They looked like they were done by the same person. My face is always drawn the same way—with my eyes crossed and my tongue sticking out. Very original.

So it *has* to be Webby. Who else hates me that much?

Unless Webby didn't draw *any* of the pictures. Maybe the prowler wants me to *think* he's Webby . . .

But if it isn't Webby, who could it be?

The only other boy who was at the dance, who could have heard those words that Hee Haw said and seen my dad dancing with everybody, was Gilbert. But it can't be Gilbert! Because:

(1) Gilbert is nice. He's annoying and yucky, but not mean. I don't think he would do something mean like vandalize my clubhouse. I don't think he is even brave enough to sneak into a girls' bathroom.
(2) Gilbert likes me. Why would someone do something mean to someone he likes?
(3) I'm pretty sure Gilbert can't draw.

That leaves as my only other suspects: all the teachers, or my dad. There's no way it's my dad. I think we can both agree to rule him out.

But the teachers? Or Mr. Unitas? That seems impossible too.

Hmmm.

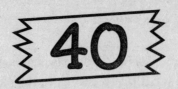

Gilbert Is a Bad Artist

Update: It wasn't Gilbert.

We had art class this afternoon, and when Mr. Strickland told us to draw the face of someone we care about, Gilbert drew me. I know it was me because the picture was labeled *Claire Warren*.

Otherwise, I never would have guessed. It didn't even look like a person. It looked like a balloon with a volcano on top erupting brown strings. Was that supposed to be my hair?

He can't draw at all, and whoever's been drawing on my wall CAN draw, at least well enough so you can tell what the picture is supposed to be.

Three days to b-day. So far not one person has RSVP'd to say that they're coming to my party.

No one will show. Same as the square dance. That's fine with me. I don't like any of them anyway.

Maybe I'll just walk to California,
Claire

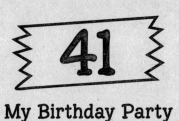

My Birthday Party

Hi Bess,

Thank you for the card you sent, and the great present! I always wanted a T-shirt with a map of the San Francisco subway system on it. Not that I knew there was a BART before, but now that I know, I can't think of anything I'd rather have.

My party is raging as we speak. Ha ha. I mean, it was supposed to start half an hour ago. My hunch was right—nobody's here.

I don't want to admit it, but I feel sad about it. I thought at least my brothers would be here, but Jim has a lacrosse game in St. Anselm. I went to look for Gaby and found him in his room with the door locked. I knocked and said, "Gabe! Don't you want any cake?"

He didn't answer. I listened at the door for a second. I heard little sniffles. He was crying.

"Gaby Baby, what's the matter?"

"Nothing! I'm not crying!"

"Come on, open the door. I'm sad and need cheering up."

He opened the door a crack.

"You do? But it's your birthday. You're supposed to be happy today."

"I know. That's the problem. Guess what? Nobody came to my party. Not even you."

"Sorry."

"The least you can do is tell me your troubles. Maybe they're so awful they'll make me feel better."

"Hey!"

"Come on. Cheer me up."

"Petey Peterson had a sleepover last night and he didn't invite me."

I should have known! Petey is Webby's little brother.

"Petey Peterson!" I exclaimed. "Is he a jerk like his older brother?"

Gabe didn't look certain. "I guess. Is Webby a jerk?"

I know it's not the kind of thing you tell a first grader, but I felt I had to warn him.

"Webby Peterson's the biggest jerk of all! I'd rather spend a whole week of Halloweens in a haunted house than sleep over at the Petersons'."

"Sam told me I missed a lot of fun. They went next door and threw eggs at *Godzilla*."

"*Godzilla*? You mean Harold Beame's boat?"

Gabe nodded.

"Harold will get them for that," I warned. I didn't like the idea of my little brother attacking boats. I didn't want him to grow up into a jerk too.

"There's more. Pete called me Gabe Snorin'."

"Gabe Snorin'? Why?"

Gabe looked like this was the worst nickname in the history of nicknames, and I felt bad for him, even if I still didn't understand.

"He says I snore. He said that's the reason I wasn't invited to the sleepover—because I snore so loud I keep everybody awake."

"Oh, I get it. *Snorin'* is supposed to rhyme with *Warren*."

The thing is, Gabe *does* snore. It's weird, for a first grader to snore so loud. He takes after Dad, I guess.

"That's so dumb," I told Gabe. "*Snorin'* doesn't really rhyme with *Warren*. I mean, it's close, but it's a stretch."

I don't think the fact that his nickname doesn't rhyme with his real name made Gabe feel better. He's sensitive. You could tell the snoring thing really hurt his feelings.

Which means that maybe he won't turn into a jerk.

He got all teary and was trying not to cry, but I saw his little body shudder with the effort. So I hugged him, and it all came rushing out.

"Aw, Gaby," I said.

"Stop calling me that. It sounds like *baby*!"

"I'm sorry. What should I call you?"

"Just Gabe. And not Gaby Baby either. That's REALLY babyish."

"I'm sorry. Gabe."

He sobbed a little longer. I sat there hugging him, half listening for the doorbell to ring. Part of me was still hoping.

"Let's go out on the porch," I suggested. "It's a really pretty day."

It is too, Bess. Remember what spring is like here? Rainy and muddy and raw for weeks and weeks, and then one day toward the end of April, the sun warms us up and the dogwoods bloom pink and white and everything looks bright and plumped-up. And it all smells so fresh and earthy and perfume-y, like just-washed horses wearing wreaths of flowers. Today is that kind of day. Perfect weather for an eleventh birthday.

Gabe said he didn't feel like going outside. He didn't want anyone to see that he was crying.

"Well, listen," I told him. "Do you think you and me are the two saddest people in the world?"

"No. Not in the whole world."

"How about the whole country?"

He thought about it a second.

"Probably not in the whole country."

"The whole state of Maryland?"

"Well, the Orioles lost last night. They're probably pretty sad today."

"Maybe we're the saddest people on Foyes Island."

He pondered that one.

"We might be," he said.

"Let's go out on the porch and see if anybody walks by who's sadder than we are. It can be like a contest!"

"Okay!"

He was already not that sad anymore.

So now we're out here on the porch, looking for sad people. Mr. Bosch walked by and said hello. He didn't seem sad. And the Timony twins rode by on their bikes, yelling "Woo woo woo!" Which doesn't sound sad.

But it's hard to tell just by looking at someone. They could be hiding it.

Wait—here come some people now. I can see them far down the street, running toward us. A mob . . . of boys. Headed this way.

Bess, gotta go.

42

Attack of the Killer Deer

Hi Bess,

It's nighttime now. Late, like eleven o'clock. I'm sitting up in my room. Since I last wrote to you, a lot has happened!

First of all . . .

Henry got charged by a deer!

It was a buck, with big horns.

What happened was, Henry and Webby and all the other boys met at Webby's house to hang out. He had told them all not to respond to my invitation, to make me think no one was coming to my party. It was a prank! All Webby's idea, of course. They would catch me off guard, and then scare me or something.

They hung out at Webby's until they got bored. Then they decided to sneak over to spy on me and play a prank. Like, maybe they could find more ways of ruining my birthday.

Their big mistake was taking the shortcut through the woods. While they were walking through, they saw a whole little family of deer.

"Freeze!" Henry whispered. He didn't want to scare them.

All the boys froze. They watched the deer. The doe kept eating grass but the buck lifted his head and looked at them steadily. Henry said it was like seeing a statue come to life—kind of cool and kind of scary.

Webby said something like, "I dare you to jump on his back and ride him."

And Henry said back something like, "What? That's impossible. Deer won't let you ride them."

Webby dared him to feed the deer a granola bar that Webby happened to have in his pocket.

Gilbert said he didn't know if deer were supposed to eat granola bars.

But Webby was like, "It won't hurt him. Go ahead. Are you chicken? Are you afraid of a shy little Bambi?"

All this time the boys were standing very still and whispering, so the deer hadn't run away yet. You know how the deer are around here—they're pretty used to people. Remember when I asked my parents if I could keep that little baby deer as a pet? The one that came to our yard every morning? Mom said it would be cruel to keep a deer in the house, but I know if I held out a carrot, that deer would have walked inside and made himself at home.

Anyway, Webby kept taunting Henry until he couldn't take it anymore. Henry unwrapped the granola bar and stuffed the wrapper in his jeans pocket. Then he took one careful step toward the deer family. The mother and baby calmly kept eating but the buck didn't take his eye off Henry. Henry said he felt like the buck was looking straight through to his soul, saying, *Go ahead, buddy. Go ahead and take another step.*

Webby also said, "Go ahead, Henry."

So Henry took another step. Then another. The doe lifted her head. She looked alarmed. She and the baby hopped away through the woods. Henry waited for the buck to follow them, but he didn't.

Webby told Henry to keep going.

Henry kept going.

He took two more steps and that's when the buck lost it. He aimed his big sharp antlers at Henry and charged!

The other boys scattered. Henry screamed, "Whoa!" and ran, but the buck was too fast for him. He bumped Henry right in the shoulder! Henry fell to the ground. The buck lifted his head and discovered his antler was caught in Henry's shirt. The buck panicked and tried to free himself, shaking his head. But every shake of his head shook Henry. Finally the shirt ripped and the buck ran away with a little piece of red T-shirt stuck to his antler.

The whole thing was very weird, the boys said.

Henry was bleeding, just a little bit, on his shoulder. The tip of the buck's antler had grazed it. It wasn't too bad a cut. He showed my dad where the buck bumped him and it was all black and blue.

"You're lucky he didn't gore you like a bull," Dad said.

Henry didn't say anything but he looked pretty shaken up.

Then Mom came out and asked, "Who's hungry?"

After all that excitement, the boys were starving. We ate pizza, and then Mom shooed us outside. We played a new game, Escape from the Killer Deer. Basically, one person is the Killer Deer, and he counts to thirty while everyone hides. The Killer Deer goes looking for victims, and if he gores you (we made a kind of antler crown out of sticks taped to a baseball cap), you're the Killer Deer.

We made Gilbert be the Killer Deer first. He counted to thirty, then tried to find me. He could have caught Zach M., Kevin, and Henry first, but no. He waited until he found me hiding behind the boat shed and chased me until he caught me. He tagged me on the back with his hand, but Webby said, "You have to GORE her with the ANTLERS." So he ducked his head and touched me gently with the antlers. I was it.

But not for long. I found Henry right where I knew he'd be—hiding inside *Swifty*.

We ran around goring each other until it got dark, and Dad called us in for cake.

Mom lit the candles and I made a wish. (I can't tell you what it is or it won't come true. However, I will say it involves a moving van driving up to your house in San Francisco.) Then I blew out the candles.

That's when I realized: The boys all came to my party after all. Maybe they didn't mean to, but it turned out kind of fun anyway. Nobody brought presents, but I didn't mind. I'm sure their presents would have been terrible.

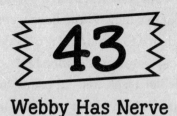

Webby Has Nerve

Monday

Hi Bess,

I'm in the clubhouse. It's lunchtime. My birthday is over. I'm officially eleven.

Yesterday and today, when I woke up in the morning, I tested myself to see if being eleven felt any different from being ten. So far, not really.

Also, Henry didn't come pick me up.

Not to drop off a present for me.

Not to walk to school with me and Gabe.

That didn't end up being different. But maybe other things are. I don't know. A surprising thing just happened. I came in here to eat lunch alone as usual. Before I had a chance to unwrap my tuna sandwich, there was a knock at the door.

Very surprising.

I froze, thinking maybe it was a trick, or a mistake. But the knock came again.

"Come in?" I called.

The door swung open, and there stood Webster Peterson.

"Aha!" I shouted. "So it IS you!"

He blinked. "What are you talking about?"

"The bathroom prowler! It's you!"

I figured this was proof that he was the one drawing mean things on my wall. Otherwise, what would he be doing there?

"I still don't know what you're talking about," Webby told me.

I showed him the pictures on my wall, the ones of me falling in the mud during the soccer game, of Starshine with *x*'s over his eyes, and the bowling and the square dance. He laughed when he saw the one I drew this morning—it showed Henry in the woods being charged by the deer.

"I wish I could draw that good," Webby told me. "I don't know who's doing it, but it's not me."

I watched his face very carefully while he said this. He looked me right in the eye, and he didn't flinch.

I have to say I believe him. He's not the prowler.

But then WHO IS??? It's driving me crazy.

You probably want to know what Webby wanted, if it wasn't to deface the clubhouse walls. He wanted something almost as bad.

"Claire," he said, "I came to ask you something."

He looked nervous, which made ME nervous. I was afraid he was going to ask me out on a date or something! Which would be insane.

But no.

Instead he said, "The spring regatta is next month, and I want to win. Will you crew for me?"

Can you believe his nerve? He asked ME, the Foyes Island junior champion two regattas in a row, to crew for HIM?

I tried to remember my manners. I stopped myself from laughing in his face.

"No," I told him. "I'm a skipper. I don't crew for anyone."

Webby shrugged. "Suit yourself. But together, we could win."

"Yeah. And without you, I can win too. I've already done it twice. So why should I crew for you?"

"I thought we'd be a good team. Unbeatable."

"Maybe so," I said. "Do YOU want to crew for ME?"

He looked shocked.

"What? I'm not going to be bossed around by anybody. Especially not a girl."

Aha! Now the REAL Webby was coming out.

"Then you're not going to win the regatta," I told him. "Now get out of the girls' bathroom."

He backed out of there like he was afraid I'd take a bite out of his head or something.

What's wrong with boys, Bess? Why are they so weird?

I don't get it.

I'm the best skipper on the island. The best junior skipper, anyway. So why wouldn't Webby be honored to be bossed around by me? What does being a girl have to do with it?

I wish it was my birthday. Everything seemed to go right then.

But I guess everyday days are harder.

Yours in solidarity,
Claire

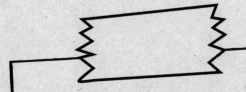

Part 4

Smuggler Joe's Treasure

June

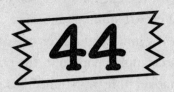

The Social Studies Fight

Dear Bess,

When does your school year end? Ours is almost over. Only three more long, hot weeks.

Mr. Harper told us we have to do a final project for social studies. It's due in two weeks—the Friday before Regatta Weekend. The project is to research some part of Foyes Island history and present a report on it to the rest of the class.

It's a group project. Mr. H. assigned the groups.

Here is my group:

Me.
Henry.
And Webby.

I don't see how this will work.

Webby has been meaner than ever. When they serve peas in the cafeteria, he saves a few in a napkin, loads them into a straw, and then shoots them at me in the hall.

Somehow, when I turn around to catch him, he's standing around in a crowd looking innocent.

But I know it's him. Right after one of his attacks, I saw him toss a crumpled napkin in the trash. I pulled it out and uncrumpled it. It was stained pea green.

That's just one example. But you know Webby. I don't have to tell you what he's like.

Maybe he's mad because I refused to crew for him. If that's true, he can go on being mad forever, I don't care.

Mr. H. told us to split up into our groups to brainstorm ideas. I have a GREAT idea for THE BEST HISTORY PROJECT EVER. Henry thinks it's a great idea too. But guess who doesn't?

Right. Webby.

Webby has his own idea for a super-great history project. He says mine is impossible!

But it's not impossible. Just because I don't know how to make it work doesn't mean it *can't* work. There's got to be a way.

Here are the two projects, Bess. You tell me which one you think is most likely to get an A.

Project 1: We tell the story of Wally the Wahoo, the biggest fish ever caught off the coast of Maryland, while showing the stuffed trophy version of the real Wally.

Project 2: We find Smuggler Joe's treasure. Or at least make a map to the treasure, so the final presentation can be a field trip to go dig it up.

Duh . . . Project 2 wins, right? I mean, which would you rather do, dig for treasure or look at a big dead fish?

Of course, Wally the Wahoo happens to be mounted in Webby's rec room, because the champion fisherman who caught Wally in 1973 happens to be Webby's grandfather, Robert Webster Peterson.

Here's how our brainstorming discussion went.

Webby started by saying, "I have the best idea. We should tell how my grandfather caught the biggest fish ever in the history of the world. It'll be so cool because we can show the fish! I've got it in my rec room."

Me and Henry exchanged glances. Then I said, "I've got an even better idea. Let's research the history of Smuggler Joe and find his treasure."

I could tell Henry liked this idea . . . but I could also tell he wasn't going to say it because he didn't want to argue with Webby.

And we all know Webby never goes down without a fight.

"That's not a good idea," he said. "It's a *dumb* idea."

"What's so dumb about it?" I asked.

"Smuggler Joe wasn't real! He's just a story people tell, like the Booger Man or the Headless Horseman."

"It's the Boogey Man, not the Booger Man."

"Wrong again, Einstein. Want me to look it up?"

"Yeah!" I said. "Let's look it up."

I thought Henry might jump in to back me up. But instead he jumped in to say, "We're getting off the subject. We're talking about Smuggler Joe, not the Boogey Man."

"See?" I said. "Boogey. I *might* accept *bogey*, but never *booger*."

Webby told me to shut up. I told him to shut up. This went back and forth for a while. Then I said, "I think Smuggler Joe was real. But even if he wasn't, it's a good topic for a history project. Foyes Island was a smugglers' port and a pirate haven a long time ago, so searching for Smuggler Joe is a good way to show our early history."

Webby wasn't swayed. "It's stupid," he insisted.

Henry asked, "Do you really think we can find the treasure?"

I nodded. "If it exists, we can find it. And if we find it, that will prove Smuggler Joe was real, and not just a legend. And that will be huge! Plus—treasure!"

"My project is better," Webby huffed. "We can call it *Wahoo! That's a Dang Big Fish!* Here's how we'll start . . ."

Webby cleared his throat and straightened an imaginary tie.

"Mr. Harper, esteemed classmates: This is the story of the biggest fish EVER CAUGHT, EVER! And we have it right here. Look how big it is!!!!"

Henry and I were silent.

Then Henry said, "Is that the whole project?"

I pushed on. "Webby, trust me, if we do my project we'll get an A, even if we don't find the treasure."

Webby decided to turn to Henry instead of trying to

answer me, saying, "Henry, you're not going to listen to this GIRL, are you?"

Henry looked really uncomfortable. Then he started to say, "Well . . ."

Webby put his hands over his ears and went, "Blah blah blah blah I can't hear you!"

"Webby," I said, "take your hands off your ears."

"I still can't hear you!"

"Webby!" I yanked his hands off his ears. "Stop it!"

"I won't stop it. You guys better do what I want—or else."

He shook his fist at us.

Such a boy thing to do!

"We're supposed to be a team," I reminded him. "Teammates don't threaten each other to get their way."

"I don't need to threaten anybody, because majority rules, right, Henry? And it's two against one. Me and Henry against you. We win. We're doing the fish story."

I was NOT going to let him get away with this. "We never took a vote!" I protested. "Henry, you're not going to vote for that dumb fish idea, are you?"

"Well . . ."

It seemed like "well . . ." was all he could say. After that he clammed up.

For the rest of the class, Webby and I fumed, and Henry looked like he was caught in a bear trap.

After class I went to the clubhouse and drew a picture of our meeting on the wall. Here it is:

To be honest, Bess, I have no idea if Smuggler Joe was real or not. I don't know where the treasure is, or how to find it, or if it even exists! I just think my idea is better. And I have to push hard to get it past Webby. I need Henry on my side.

This fight isn't over. I'm going to start working on finding Smuggler Joe's gold.

First stop: the library.

On the trail,
Claire

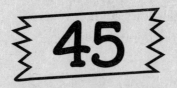

The Ghost of Smuggler Joe

Dear Bess,

I had a wild adventure today. The kind of thing that people might not believe, if I told them. But I know I can count on you to believe me, because you're my best friend. You know I don't lie or make up stories.

Wait until you hear this.

I woke up feeling sad about Henry. I know he likes my idea better than Webby's, but I can't get him to tell Webby that.

I moped around the house feeling friendless and miserable.

"It's too beautiful a day for moping," Mom said. "Why don't you go outside and enjoy it?"

Mom was right. It was sunny and warm out, so I decided to go out for a ride. I saddled up Starshine and we took off into the woods. As soon as I sat in the saddle, I began to feel better. Starshine does that for me.

I rode slowly along the path to Eliot Point, singing Starshine's Good Morning theme song. Because it rained a lot this spring, the ground is soft and dark, and the trees are so green and full that the path looks like a glowing undersea tunnel. I reached up to touch the cool leaves while Starshine ambled along underneath me. We were both feeling calm and carefree.

You know how Starshine is: Nothing bothers him. He can't jump high like some horses but he's steady and not easily startled.

Most of the time.

But there's one thing that scares the willies out of him.

And that thing is snakes.

So while we were heading calmly through the woods, all of a sudden Starshine snorted and tensed up underneath me. A long black snake wriggled across the path, right in front of us. Starshine stopped dead. He wouldn't move.

I tugged on his reins. "Come on, Starshine. The snake won't hurt us. Just step over it."

But the snake lifted its head and hissed at us. That's all it took.

Starshine reared up. Then he put his head down and charged.

I clung to his neck as he ran down the path. "Starshine, stop!" I cried. I yanked on the reins. But he was spooked.

So he kept running.

We rounded a curve. Up ahead a huge fallen tree lay across the path. Starshine galloped straight for it.

He was going to jump!

And he's not a jumper. Not at all.

I sat up in the saddle and prepared to sail over that gigantic tree. But Starshine ducked his head and stopped short. I went flying off his back and landed with a thud on the other side of the tree trunk.

Everything went black for a second.

I opened my eyes. Little white pinpricks of light clouded my vision. After they cleared up, I saw Starshine's head peering at me over the fallen tree trunk. The trunk was so big it came up to his haunches. He never would have made it over if he'd tried to jump it.

I tried to sit up, but I felt dizzy, so I stayed on the ground. "I'm okay!" I told Starshine. I could tell he was worried about me.

Then I heard a rustling through the trees. Starshine's eyes rested on something behind me. I tried to sit up again to look, but my head hurt, just a little, and I couldn't do it.

"What is it, Starshine?" I asked, even though I knew he couldn't answer me.

Swish swish swish—the rustling sound got louder, closer . . .

"Hello?" I called. "Is someone out there?"

I groped around until my hand landed on the largest stick I could find. I held it up, weapon at the ready.

I saw the leaves moving first. Then some tawny brown-and-white fur. Then a flash of red.

It was the Killer Deer! A piece of Henry's T-shirt was still stuck on his antler.

I tried to lift my head, but it felt so heavy. I waved my big stick.

"Try to get me, Killer Deer! I'll bonk you right on the antlers!"

The deer stopped a few feet away and stared down at me where I lay on the ground.

I lay perfectly still. Isn't that what you're supposed to do if a bear comes near you? I didn't know if it would work for a killer deer too, but I didn't have much choice.

And then—Bess, I swear this is true—the deer moved its little deer mouth, and words came out.

I'm not kidding. The deer talked.

He said, "I am the ghost of Smuggler Joe."

I just stared in a stunned silence.

The Killer Deer continued. "Do not fear me. I won't hurt you. I didn't mean to hurt that boy, your friend. I was only trying to talk to him, but he panicked and then his shirt got caught on my antler. Will you take it off, by the way?"

He had a weird, squeaky voice. I don't know what I thought a deer's voice would sound like, but in case you're wondering, it's kind of breathy and high.

My own voice sounded a little strange when I said, "Um . . ."

The deer stepped forward and gently tilted his head down so that I could reach his antlers without getting up. I pulled the piece of red fabric off his horn. I thought I heard him sigh with relief.

"Thank you," he said.

"I don't understand. Are you a deer or a ghost?"

"I'm the ghost of Joe, temporarily using the body of a deer. I can't speak to humans without a body. But I have been trying to give you a message! Haven't you seen me lurking around your boathouse?"

"I thought that was you! But I couldn't be sure. You're so . . . shadowy."

Killer Deer/Joe shook his head from side to side. "I can't help it! It's the ghost thing, not having a body and all. It's hard to make your presence felt when you've been dead as long as I have."

"So what's the message?" I asked.

"It's about my treasure—"

Just then Starshine neighed, really loudly. The Killer Deer tensed up like he was afraid. Starshine neighed again. He scared the deer, who leaped away through the woods.

"Starshine!" I cried. "He was about to tell me something very important!"

Of course NOW Starshine was quiet. He looked sorry. I guess horses can't help neighing at deer, and deer can't help getting spooked and running off, even if they have a human ghost temporarily living inside them.

I sat up. My head felt a little better now. I stood up carefully . . . I was okay. I waited a minute to see if the deer would return. The woods were quiet.

"Joe!" I tried. "Come back!"

Nothing.

"Joe!"

A breeze rustled the leaves. That was the only sound. The Killer Deer didn't return.

I climbed up onto Starshine's back and we rode slowly home. He seemed a little jittery from the whole experience. To tell you the truth, I was too.

But, Bess, I swear this really happened. I had proof.

I was holding the piece of Henry's red T-shirt in my hand.

Henry Is Skeptical

I led Starshine back to the stable, then went inside the house. Mom was sitting at the kitchen table.

"Are you okay?" she asked. "You have leaves in your hair."

I reached up and plucked some leaves off my head. I hadn't realized they were there.

"Starshine saw a snake and lost it," I told her. "I fell off. But I'm okay! The ground was really soft."

"What?" Mom jumped to her feet. "Are you really okay? Did you hit your head?"

"Not very hard. I'm fine."

She stared into my eyes. "Do you feel dizzy? Do you have a headache?"

"No," I insisted.

She frowned. "I'm taking you to the clinic anyway, just to be sure."

"Mom, I promise I'm fine!" I wanted to go see Henry and tell him what happened. Maybe he'd want his piece of T-shirt back. Not that it's of much use to him, but you never know.

Mom herded me out to the car and drove me to the clinic anyway. Dr. Stacy checked me out. She asked me a bunch of questions like how many fingers she was holding up and shined a light in my eyes and said I looked okay to her.

"Whew, that's good," Mom said, and we drove home.

As soon as I got out of the car, I whistled for Bruno and walked over to Henry's house. His mother said he and his dad had gone sailing.

I took Bruno with me to the dock and saw their boat way out in the river, almost as far as the bay. I sat down with Bruno and waited.

It was warm out today, but the air still gets chilly when the sun goes down. I sat with my hand warming on Bruno's furry back, watching the water drift by, the boats in the distance. The oystermen puttered by in their skiff. Zach's and Webby's dads waved to me from a fishing boat. The sun floated down in the west and changed color, from lemony to butterscotchy to blood orange. The water changed color too, blue-green to silver-blue to blue-black.

I don't know if you know this about me, Bess, but sometimes, when there's no one else around, I talk to Bruno. So there I was sitting on the dock by myself and I told Bruno all about Henry and why we were waiting for him. He thumped his tail, which always makes me think he understands what I'm saying. Mom says I'm just imagining it, but I don't think so.

I told Bruno how much I miss you, and how lonely I've been since you left, and how glad I am that at least I have him and Starshine to keep me company. I love animals but they're not the same as people. I need animal friends AND people friends to be happy. My friends can be girls or boys. I really don't care about that. As long as they like me and I can be myself around them.

Maybe that's why it's been hard around the boys since you left, Bess. They don't seem to want me to be myself. It's like they're afraid my girlishness will bring out their girlishness. I know they all have a little bit in them. Henry does. Remember that time all three of us slept over at your house, and you wanted to paint your toenails acid green, and then I wanted to too, and then Henry let us paint his toenails too? And we were laughing at how good he looked with acid-green toenails. And he liked it! But that was last year, when we were only ten. Everything gets different when you're older.

I watched Henry's boat tack back and forth, and I could tell his dad was teaching him things for the regatta.

He wants to win this time, I thought.

It was beginning to get dark when Henry and his dad sailed up to the dock. Bruno jumped up and barked and wagged his tail. Mr. Long said, "What did we do to deserve this welcoming committee?"

"I just wanted to talk to Henry for a minute."

Henry's dad nodded at him, like, *Go ahead, I'll catch up*. Henry jumped off the boat, tied it to the dock, and walked down the path with me and Bruno.

174

I told him that the ghost of Smuggler Joe had just visited me in the form of the Killer Deer who'd attacked him a couple of months ago. I think you know Henry well enough to be able to picture the look on his face when I said this, but just in case you *can't* picture it, I'll draw it for you.

"Claire," he said, "I think you've lost your mind."

Honestly, I could understand why he might think that. But instead of backing down, I said, "Oh yeah?"

I pulled out the piece of red cloth.

I went on. "Is this, or is this not, part of the T-shirt you were wearing when the Killer Deer attacked you?"

Henry gasped. "It is!"

"See? Now do you believe me?"

Henry shook his head. "Not really. Maybe it fell off the deer and you found it in the woods."

"But I didn't!"

"Maybe you hit your head when you fell and this was all a dream."

"Maybe. But when we find Joe's treasure, that will prove my story is true. So we might as well just assume there was a Smuggler Joe, he had treasure, and we're going to find it."

"Okay . . ." Henry said. "You're idea is better than Webby's. I admit it. But . . . *you* have to convince him."

I didn't even flinch.

"Easy peasy!" I promised Henry. "I'll take on Webby all by myself, and you don't have to do a thing to help . . . on one condition."

"What is it?"

"Will you crew for me in the spring regatta?"

He hesitated.

"I saw you and your dad out there. You looked good."

"Thanks, but . . . crew for you?"

I didn't see how this was so hard to understand. "Yes. I'm the skipper. But if you crew for me, I think we'll win."

Henry thought it over.

"You want to win, don't you?" I asked him.

"Sure I do."

"So? Say yes."

Henry smiled. He hasn't smiled at me in so long!

"It *would* be nice to win," he admitted. "And Webby's so bossy—even more bossy than you." He paused to think about it for a few more seconds. "Okay, I'll do it."

We shook on it.

Then Henry asked, "What about Gilbert?"

Gilbert. I'm afraid he's expecting to crew for me again. And I'm afraid he'll be disappointed. But Henry is a much better sailor than Gilbert. I don't have to explain every little thing to Henry. He just knows what to do.

"Maybe he can crew for Webby," I suggested.

Henry laughed. "I don't think so."

"Well, I'll figure out something. Do you want to practice tomorrow? We'd better get out on the water—we've got a title to defend."

That's how it happened, Bess. Henry and I are a team again.

I'm so glad.

I told you it was a wild adventure, right?

Claire

Fish, Fish, Fish

Dear Bess,

During social studies today, Mr. H. told us to split up into our groups to work on our projects.

"By now you should have settled on the subject of your project," he said. "Have you all decided what you're going to do?"

Everybody nodded and kind of murmured yes . . . except for me, Henry, and Webby.

Mr. Harper continued, "If any group hasn't decided what their project is going to be yet, raise your hands."

I looked at Henry and Webby, like, *Shouldn't we be raising our hands?* Webby glared at us. We got the message: *Raise your hands and I'll shoot peas at you every chance I get.*

So we didn't.

Mr. Harper smiled. "Okay, good. Get to work!"

Reluctantly, Webby, Henry, and I gathered at Henry's desk.

Cocking his head to make sure Mr. Harper couldn't hear him, Webby said, "We didn't need to raise our hands because we know what our project is. The Fish History."

"Actually—" I started.

Webby tried to stop me with a Glare of Death. I went on.

"No, really, Webby. This is big."

This got me a Glare of the Apocalypse.

To which I said, "Tell him, Henry."

Henry didn't like the spotlight turning on him. "*You* tell him," he said. "We made a deal, remember? And anyway, it was *your* vision."

"Vision?" Webby jumped in. "That sounds fishy, ha ha. Get it?"

Henry nodded. "Good one, Web."

Hmph. Whose side is he on?

"It wasn't a vision," I told them. "It really happened."

Webby looked at me like I was a fly that wouldn't get away from his ear. "Okay, tell me. What really happened?"

"I saw the ghost of Smuggler Joe! He came to me in the body of the Killer Deer. And he told me where the treasure is buried! Or he was about to, when Starshine scared him off—"

"Uh-huh," Webby interrupted. "That's totally believable."

"It's true! I swear."

"Well, guess what. I saw a giant talking wahoo fish yesterday and you know what he told me? He told me he's the ghost of the biggest fish anybody ever caught off the coast of Maryland, and he wants us to do our social studies project about him. If we don't, he's going to smack us to death with his giant slimy fish tail!"

Henry and I stared at him. Henry blinked.

"What?" Webby said. "It's just as believable as your dumb story."

"But my story is true. If we prove that Smuggler Joe really lived back in the 1700s, we will make island history! And we'll get an A in social studies for sure."

Webby gave Henry a doubtful glance and asked him, "Are you in on this Smuggler Joe idea too?"

My heart dropped. I thought there was no way Henry was going to go for it now. Not when he was face-to-face with Webby.

But Henry surprised me. "It's a good idea. It's not going to be easy, but if we can do it, it will be amazing!"

Webby was outraged. "But you're my friend! You're supposed to be on my side! Not on *her* side."

The way Webby said "her" sounded like he was about to spit.

"I'm not on anybody's side," Henry replied. "I just want to do a good project."

"Hey!" I said. "You were *my* friend first."

Henry knew he had a mess on his hands. "This isn't about friendship," he assured both me and Webby. "It's a school project."

He kicked me under the table. The meaning of this kick was unclear. I took it to mean, *Yes, we're friends again, but let's not set off Webby.*

But I could be wrong.

Webby covered his ears and started saying, "Fish fish fish fish. Fish fish fish fish. Fish fish fish fish . . ."

"He's not listening to you," Henry told me.

"I can see that."

I yanked one of Webby's hands off his ear and told him, "We're doing Smuggler Joe whether you help us or not. If we get an A, you'll get an A too, without doing any work. Okay?"

Webby put his hand back over his ear. "No. Fish fish fish fish . . ."

Mr. Harper strolled over to see how we were doing.

"Is there a problem over here?" he asked.

"No," I said.

"This is our creative process," Henry assured him.

"Fish fish fish fish!" Webby said.

Mr. Harper looked skeptical. "Well, okay. But if you need help, don't be afraid to come to me."

He walked away.

I turned to Henry. "Now that we have our subject figured out, we need to get to work. We're behind everyone else. And I'm not sure Webby's going to be much help."

We both turned to look at him.

"Fish!" he said defiantly.

It looked like the two of us would have to do our three-person project . . . and in record time.

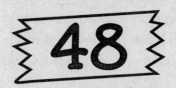

48

To the Lighthouse

Henry and I rode our bikes to the Foyes Island Historical Society after school. Webby refused to go with us. He should have come, because the first thing we saw when we walked in was a giant picture of his grandfather holding Wally the Wahoo in 1973.

I'm glad Webby didn't come with us actually. That picture might have strengthened his case.

"You know what?" Henry asked as we passed under the picture. "The acronym for the Foyes Island Historical Society is FIHS, which is an anagram of FISH."

"That is not helpful," I told him. "It's totally meaningless and a coincidence."

"I just noticed it, that's all."

I don't know if you ever went to the historical society when you lived here, Bess. It's in the lighthouse at the end of Eliot Point. It's not very big. Foyes Island history goes back five hundred years, but not a whole lot has happened here over those five hundred years. Basically, back then people farmed and sailed and fished and dredged for oysters and caught crabs. We do all those things now. Not that much has changed.

The shape of the island has changed some, though. There's a section in the historical society called *Hurricanes, Droughts, Floods, and Storms* that talks about some of the biggest natural disasters in the island's history. There's a map comparing the shape of the island now to how it looked when the first English explorers landed in the 1600s. Storms have washed away a lot of land over the years. Eliot Point used to stick way out into the bay!

There are also pictures from the more recent hurricanes. The worst was Hurricane Agnes in 1972. The marina was under five feet of water! Some people's houses washed away and boats blew out to sea. We saw a picture of the wreckage of the Three Fiddlers Pub, which stood on our property before my grandparents bought that land and built the house we live in now.

The most exciting period was definitely the American Revolution, which was Smuggler Joe's time. There's a little diorama in the back of the historical society, behind a glass window, labeled *Pirates, Smugglers, and Shipwrecks*. It shows the marina with lots of big old-fashioned schooners and sloops and clipper ships anchored in the port, and little rowboats filled with bags labeled CONTRABAND, rowed by guys in pirate hats.

Next to the diorama is a panel labeled *The Legend of Smuggler Joe*. I took a picture of it. Here's what it says:

THE LEGEND OF SMUGGLER JOE

According to Foyes Island legend, the most devious and successful smuggler during the 1700s was a mysterious man known as Smuggler Joe. When hard-to-get provisions such as sugar or tea suddenly appeared in the Foyes Island Market, people whispered that it had been sneaked past the British blockades by Smuggler Joe. He was said to frequent the Three Fiddlers Pub, and the pub's manager, Josie Maloney, claimed to be his close confidante. But whenever anyone—especially the police or government agents—went looking for him, he was not to be found.

In 1789, a small ship wrecked just off the coast of Foyes Island. No one survived, but several empty wooden chests washed ashore. They were the kind of chests often used to hold gold and other treasures. Did the treasure fall out and sink to the bottom of the bay? No trace of it was ever found. Nor was Smuggler Joe ever seen again. Perhaps he'd died on the doomed ship. If he was a real person—which no one has ever proven—that fate seems likely.

But what about the empty treasure chests? People said that Joe had buried his smuggler's spoils somewhere on the island. They speculated that he had been coming ashore to dig up his treasure, put it in the empty chests, and take it away with him to the Caribbean. But he died before he could get to it.

To this day, many people believe that his ghost haunts the island, guarding his buried treasure.

Ever since then, when strange things happen on Foyes Island, people blame it on Smuggler Joe's ghost.

I was a little spooked out, but Henry didn't seem as bothered.

"There's nothing here we don't already know," he said.

I played it cool. "Yeah," I said. "I wish they'd explain why I keep seeing weird shadows around the boat shed."

"Weird shadows?"

I nodded. "And sometimes I think I see a face in the window. Mom says it's Joe, but I know she's teasing me."

If Webby had been there, I'm sure he would have been teasing me too. But not Henry.

Henry was taking me seriously.

"Maybe she isn't teasing you," he said. "Maybe she means it."

"What are you saying?"

Henry smiled. "I'm saying, let's go to your house and see what we see!"

The Boat Shed

We rode back to my house. It was getting dark. That's the most shadowy time, right before night falls.

"Where did you see this face?" Henry asked me.

I pointed to the window in the boat shed door. Henry studied it carefully. He walked around the outside of the shed. Then he went inside. I flicked on the light.

Henry tested some of the floorboards with his shoe. A few of them were loose.

"Let's say you saw a ghost in the window. Why would he be here?"

"I don't know. I thought he wanted a dry place to sleep."

Henry shook his head. "Ghosts don't sleep. And they don't get wet."

Mr. Expert! "How do you know?" I asked.

"It just makes sense."

"If you say so," I said. But I wasn't convinced.

His question started jingle-jangling in my mind, bouncing around through my brain cells, lighting up new thoughts. Why would a ghost hang around my boat shed?

Maybe he was guarding his treasure.

"Henry . . . are you thinking what I'm thinking?"

"Maybe. Are you thinking that it smells like your dad's baking brownies for dessert?"

"No." I sniffed the air. It smelled like chocolate. "But I do think he's making brownies."

Henry liked that answer. "Can I stay for dinner?" he asked.

Just like old times! I was excited, but I didn't want to spook Henry. So I played it cool. "Yes. But we're getting off track."

"Right."

"IF the shadows I've seen are the ghost of Smuggler Joe, and IF he haunts the island to guard his treasure, then MAYBE his treasure—"

Henry kicked up a loose floorboard.

"Claire, look at this."

"—is buried somewhere around the shed!"

"I already guessed you were going to say that."

"I know. I just had to finish the sentence out loud."

We lifted up the floorboard. The one next to it was loose too, and the one next to that. They were easy to lift.

"What's under here?" Henry asked.

I didn't have an answer. I'd never looked before.

We both looked now. Underneath was nothing but dirt. I got a flashlight off the tool shelf and shined it on the ground.

"It's just dirt," I said, disappointed.

But Henry was still looking. "What's that shiny thing?" he asked.

Something glimmered in the beam of the flashlight, something mostly covered by the soil. I reached down and brushed some dirt away.

"It's a metal loop," I reported.

I got a spade and we started digging more. The metal loop was attached to a rusty chain. And the rusty chain was attached to something buried under the shed.

Henry couldn't believe his eyes, and neither could I.

"Claire, I think there's something down there," he said.

"So do I," I agreed.

"We'll have to pull up more floorboards!"

I knew he was right. And I also knew that I couldn't tear the shed apart without permission, treasure or no treasure.

"We better ask Dad first," I told Henry.

I went into the house to ask Dad, but everyone else— Mom and Dad and Jim and Gabe—heard what I was up to, so they all came out to see the metal loop and the rusty chain. Mom looked at Dad. Dad looked at Mom.

"Go for it, kids," Mom said.

"But wait until tomorrow," Dad added. "It will be easier to work in the daylight."

"Dad! No!" I protested. "We have to do it now!"

But Dad wouldn't budge. "If that chain leads to treasure, it's been there for a long time. It can wait one more day."

So I had to go to bed and wait to see what's under there until tomorrow. It's impossible to sleep. I'm dying of curiosity!

What if I'm right, Bess? What if we found Smuggler Joe's treasure?

More news tomorrow,
Claire

To the Finder of This Map

Dear Bess,

Today was the big dig day. I got up early and called Henry. He came over right after breakfast. We went into the shed and started digging. A few minutes later, Webby arrived.

I was surprised, to say the least.

But Webby acted like it was the most normal thing in the world. "I'm here!" he said. "We can start digging now. Hey! You started without me!"

"How did you find out about this?" I asked.

I may have sounded a little hostile.

Henry turned away and started digging harder.

"Henry told me last night," Webby said, confirming my suspicion.

"He's on our team," Henry said. "He should know what we're doing."

"Okay," I said. Then I locked my eyes on Webby. "But this means you agree that our social studies project is about Smuggler Joe and not about Wally the Wahoo, right?"

Webby stood firm. "That depends on what's buried under this here boat shed."

Ugh.

I didn't feel like arguing. I felt like digging.

We dug around that rusty chain for half an hour until my shovel hit something hard.

"I think this is it!" I called.

I ran inside to get Dad and Jim to help us dig out whatever was there. We saw a bit of old wood. We saw a strip of rusty iron. The strips of wood and iron began to look like a small chest.

Dad was so excited. "I don't believe it! I think this really *is* a treasure chest."

We dug and dug until we could pull the chest out of the ground. It was very heavy. It was closed with a big lock that was so old and rusty Dad broke it pretty easily with a hammer.

By this time the shed was crowded. Mom and Gabe had come out to see what we'd found. We made everybody promise to keep the whole thing a secret until we knew what we had.

Mom rubbed her hands and said, "Here we go!"

"Claire, would you like to do the honors?" Dad asked.

I knelt beside the chest and lifted the lid. It was very heavy.

Inside were some wads of cloth.

"What is it?" Gabe asked, peering in. "A bunch of old clothes?"

I rummaged through the cloth until I felt something hard. Nestled among the fabric was a glass bottle stoppered with a cork.

Webby sighed. "That's it? An old bottle. Great job, Claire."

"Wait—there's something inside!" I announced. "A piece of paper!"

I tugged on the cork but it wouldn't come out. Dad got some pliers and yanked it out of the bottle. I pulled out a rolled up piece of paper. The paper was yellow and crumbly around the edges and very delicate. I carefully unrolled it.

It was a map of Foyes Island! It showed Eliot Point, and the lighthouse, and some houses that are gone now and a few others that are still standing. One spot on Eliot Point was marked with a big *X*.

I'm going to try to draw it for you here.

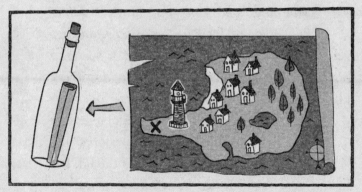

I gasped.

"It's a treasure map!" I told everyone.

"Let me see!" Henry called out. "Wow!"

Webby played it cooler (although I could tell he was excited too). "What?" he said. "You mean we have to do more digging?"

"There's something else here," I said.

There was another piece of parchment under the map. It had shaky, faded writing on it that was hard to read. Mom helped me piece it together. Here's what it said:

> To the Finder of This Map—
>
> I, Joseph Tarbox of Foyes Island, Maryland, do hereby declare that the treasure buried on the spot marked herewith belongs to me. In the event of my demise, if ye be an honest man or woman, deliver this map or the treasure, whichever ye have found, to my good friend Josephine Maloney, who runs the Three Fiddlers Pub. Joe and Josie we are, two scalawags who mean no harm to anyone.
>
> The chest contains the spoils of my hard work, a good score of years of smuggling tea and sugar and other goods to the hungry fisherfolk of Foyes, which earned me the affectionate moniker of Smuggler Joe. I carry the name proudly. A smuggler I am and always will be.
>
> Signed this 3rd day of September, 1788
> Joseph Tarbox

Bess, I couldn't believe my luck. This was what I'd been hoping for! Proof that Smuggler Joe was a real person! AND a treasure map!

"NOW can we do Smuggler Joe for our project?" I asked Webby.

This time his answer wasn't *fishy* at all.

"Okay, okay," he said. "Let's find the treasure!"

Henry pointed to the X on the map. "All we have to do is go right THERE."

Joe had marked an X at the end of a finger of Eliot Point that stuck out into the Chesapeake Bay. The way Eliot Point was drawn didn't look quite right. I don't remember ever seeing that finger jutting into the water like that.

Dad studied the map. He frowned and showed it to Mom, asking her what she thought.

Mom shook her head. "Uh-oh. No. Uh-oh."

"What? What's uh-oh?" I asked.

"I don't think that spot is there anymore."

It was Webby who asked the next question. "What do you mean, that spot isn't there?"

"The end of Eliot Point washed away a long time ago," Dad explained. "I think it was Hurricane Agnes, wasn't it, honey?"

Hurricane Agnes. I had just read about it at the historical society.

Mom nodded. "That's what my parents told me. Hurricane Agnes flooded half the island, knocked down a bunch of buildings, and wiped the end of Eliot Point clear off the map. I think it was in 1972."

"But the treasure could still be there," I said. "It might be underwater! Let's go see."

Dad looked so sad when he said, "I doubt it's there. It probably washed out to sea. But when we give these documents to the state historical society, maybe they'll send divers down there to look for it."

"The historical society! No!" Webby cried out. "We found this stuff! We need it for our social studies project."

"I think this is kind of a big deal," Mom said. "Historians will want to see what you found."

"Maybe they'll let you show them to your class once they've had a look," Dad consoled. "You can certainly take pictures of everything and show those."

We put everything in ziplock bags to protect them from the elements. Henry, Webby, and I spent the rest of the afternoon figuring out what we're going to say in our presentation.

It's going to blow Mr. Harper's mind!

Your favorite treasure hunter,
Claire

History Day

Dear Bess,

Today was Foyes Island History Day. We presented our projects, and guess whose was the best? I'll describe them and then you tell me.

Calvin, Kevin, and the Zachs did a presentation called *Jerry Jawbreak: The Greatest Person Who Ever Lived on Foyes Island*, about that guy Jerry Jardine, who became a famous professional wrestler. Remember old Mr. Jardine, who sits in a rocking chair on his porch with a shotgun on his lap, yelling at kids to keep off his property? Jerry is his son. He's the most famous person who ever grew up here. The highlight of the presentation was when Calvin and Kevin reenacted the 2004 World Wrestling Championship in which Chester the Chomper shoved a six-inch nail up Jerry Jawbreak's nose. Calvin, as Jerry, howled in pain, but kept on fighting with the nail sticking out of his nose. He won the championship. Calvin and those guys acted the whole thing out. They didn't use a real nail—they made a pretend one out of gray construction paper. The grossest part was when

Calvin pulled the nail OUT of his nose. The whole class went, "Eewwww!"

Then there was Gilbert's project. Nobody wanted to work with Yucky G. I felt sorry for him. Zach R. had been assigned to his team, but he defected to the Jerry Jawbreak group. Mr. Harper said that wasn't allowed, but Gilbert said he didn't mind.

He stood up in front of the class all by himself and said, "My project is called *The Only Girl in School: The Claire Warren Story*."

I had no idea his social studies project was about ME! I was shocked.

Basically, it was about how this was the first time in the history of Foyes Island Elementary that there has been only one girl in the whole school.

I'm making history just by existing.

This is what Gilbert said:

"Foyes Island was first settled by the English in 1681. For a long time people on the island didn't go to school. They just farmed and fished and struggled to survive. In the 1700s, if kids wanted to go to school, they had to take a ferry to St. Anselm. Finally, in 1823, the people of Foyes opened their own school. It had seven pupils, four boys and three girls. I went to the library and looked up the school records, and they show that every year since then, there have always been at least two girls at the Foyes Island School—until this year.

"That means that someone in our class—Claire Warren—is making history!

"She has made island history in other ways too. She is a top scorer on the soccer team. She played more parts in a single holiday play than anybody ever has before. She has won the junior regatta twice in a row, and this weekend she might win again. That will make three times in a row, which no one else has ever done.

"In conclusion, I just want to say that Claire Warren is amazing. Thank you for your attention. The end."

He sat down. The boys clapped politely. Henry clapped more enthusiastically and even whistled. So that was nice.

Mr. Harper seemed impressed. "Very good, Gilbert," he said. "Claire, you're part of history! How does that feel?"

It feels like everyone's looking at me right now, I thought. But what I said was, "Okay, I guess."

"Great," Mr. Harper said. "You're up next!"

Webby, Henry, and I went to the front of the room.

"Our project is called *Smuggler Joe Was a Real Person and We Have Proof*," I announced to the class. "Here's what happened. I kept seeing a face near our boat shed. It turned out to be a ghost—the Ghost of Smuggler Joe. That gave Henry an idea."

"And me," Webby butted in. "This was my idea too."

I was about to say something to *that*, but Henry stepped in and continued the presentation as we'd planned it. "Everyone knows the Legend of Smuggler Joe. His ghost haunts the island to guard his treasure. I figured, if his ghost was haunting Claire's boat shed, that must be where the treasure was."

"So we pulled up the floorboards and started digging," I said. "And we found a chest!"

The class was so excited! Mr. Harper had A-pluses in his eyes. And it got even better when Henry proclaimed, "And inside the chest was . . . this!"

I unrolled the treasure map and held it up for everyone to see. The boys gasped. Mr. Harper spread out the map and the letter on his desk so everyone could look closely. He made sure no one touched them because they were so delicate.

Webby pointed to a spot on the map.

"That's where my grandfather, Robert Webster Peterson, caught the biggest fish ever. I just thought I'd add that since we're talking about local history."

"Thank you, Webby," Mr. Harper said politely. "Good to know."

I continued with our presentation. "We told the historical society what we found. They drove straight over to our house to look at the boat shed and see if there are any more artifacts buried there. So our boat shed is kind of a mess right now. They also said they might send divers out to Eliot Point to see if they can find the treasure! They don't think they'll find anything, but they said it's worth a look."

The class couldn't stop talking about our discovery. Everybody else got As, but we got an A++. Mr. Harper said he's never seen such good teamwork.

If only he knew the truth. Worst teamwork ever! But it turned out pretty well in the end.

Another Mystery Solved

We had lunch after social studies. I went to the clubhouse with my lunchbox. Before eating, I drew some pictures.

First my fall in the woods, with the Killer Deer talking to me.

Then the discovery of Smuggler Joe's treasure map.

Then three scenes from social studies: the boys acting out Jerry Jawbreak's championship fight, Gilbert declaring me part of island history, and our presentation of the treasure map.

While I drew, there was a knock at the door.

Strange. Only one person had ever knocked at the clubhouse door before: Webby. That time he had the nerve to ask me to crew for him. I hoped this wasn't Webby again, with some new way to insult me.

I opened the door. There stood Henry.

"Hey," he said. "Aren't you coming to lunch?"

"What do you mean?" I asked.

"I mean, you know, that meal we eat after breakfast and before dinner?"

"I know what lunch is. I mean, I always have lunch here."

"In the *bathroom*?"

"It's not just a bathroom. It's my clubhouse. Haven't you noticed that I haven't been to the cafeteria, like, all year?"

Henry blushed. "Um, yes, I guess I kind of noticed." He looked around a bit in a really obvious way. "It's nice in here."

"I like it."

I dropped the blue pencil I'd been drawing with. Henry leaned down to pick it up . . . and three markers fell out of his pocket.

The marker colors looked just like the ones that had been used by the prowler who broke in and drew mean things!

Henry hurried to pick up the markers, but it was too late. I had already spotted them.

"You're the prowler!" I accused.

Henry tried to act confused. "What? What are you talking about?"

"You sneaked in here and drew on the walls."

He didn't say anything. But he turned BRIGHT red.

"Why did you do it?" I asked.

The best answer he had to that was, "Um . . ."

He looked down at the floor and blinked fast.

Then he looked back up at me and said, "I'm sorry, Claire. I feel bad about the way I acted this year."

I crossed my arms and aimed my stinkiest stink eye at him. "Why DID you act so weird all year? Why did you stop walking to school with me?"

"I was going to come pick you up on the first day, just like always. But remember the day before? The barbecue at the dock?"

He meant the end-of-summer crab feast. Where I ate so much corn on the cob and watermelon I thought my stomach would explode.

"What about it?" I asked him now.

Before he could answer, I knew. Henry and I had been hanging out together at the crab feast all day long. Just like you and me and Henry did last year, and the year before, and like we would have this year if you'd been there. But you weren't there, so it was just me and Henry. And somehow, that looked different.

"Afterward, I met Webby and the other guys at Ike's Ice Cream, and he started teasing me about you. And all the other guys joined in. They said you were my girlfriend."

"But that's not true!"

"I know. I told them, we're good friends. Best friends, even. But that's all. But Webby wouldn't let it go. He started singing this song he made up, 'Claire likes Henry, Henry likes Claire, they go together like a cuss and a swear . . .'"

"That's dumb," I pointed out. "It doesn't even make sense."

Henry gave me a look and I knew—it didn't matter if it made sense or not. The damage was done.

"All the boys were singing that," he said. "And then Webby told me if I showed up at school with you in the morning they were going to hold a wedding ceremony for us at recess to make it official."

I gasped. "Ack!"

"I didn't want that. And I knew you wouldn't like it either. You wouldn't—right?"

"No!"

I was horrified. That would have been so embarrassing. A wedding!

"So, in a way," Henry continued, "I was avoiding you for your sake."

Nice try, I thought.

"Hold on just a second," I told him. "Don't try to pin this on me. You were spineless, that's what you were. Instead of telling Webby he could think what he wants, you let him tell you what to do."

Henry's red face was now going pale. "Yeah, you're right. I was spineless. I felt like I had to prove I wasn't your boyfriend, or they'd never believe me. That's why I drew those mean pictures on your wall."

"So you sneaked into my clubhouse?"

I hate to think of our sacred clubhouse being violated by the presence of enemy boys.

Henry nodded.

"Webby too?" I asked. "And the other guys?"

Too horrible to imagine.

"No, I didn't let them in. I told them if we got caught it would be bad. Unitas would use our heads for basketball trophies."

"So how did they know you did it?" I challenged.

"I took pictures on my phone to show them."

His words sank into me like a punch in the stomach. Henry, my old friend, OUR old friend, has betrayed me for almost the whole school year. He has let me be lonely and friendless, pounded with dodge balls and jeered at. AND he sneaked into my private clubhouse and defaced the walls.

But now he was telling me why. He was telling me the truth. And he was sorry. I could see it in his face.

"Will you forgive me?" he asked.

I hesitated. I stalled. I made him wait for my answer. After all, it had been a long, hard year.

Then, at last, I answered him.

"I will forgive you," I said.

Bess, you should have seen the look on his face. He brightened up like a sunflower after you water it.

"We've got a race to win tomorrow," I reminded him. "We can't go out there as enemies."

"No we can't," Henry agreed. "We're a team!"

"Yes. We're a team."

We shook hands.

Then Henry said something I didn't realize I'd been waiting almost a year for him to say: "Why don't you come to lunch now? If you want to. I saved you a seat at my table, next to me."

"Thank you," I replied. "I will."

I left the clubhouse and took my lunch to the cafeteria. I sat next to Henry and no one bothered me except Webby, who couldn't resist throwing bread balls at me every once in a while.

I didn't really mind.

I've found my table,
Claire

I Make History

Dear Bess,

Take out the school picture of me that I sent you a few months ago. Set it in front of you.

Now:

Guess who won the Foyes Island junior regatta for a HISTORIC THIRD TIME IN A ROW?!!!!

(Pick up my picture and look at it.)

That's right. YOU'RE LOOKING AT HER!

Oh yeah oh yeah oh YEAH!

And, oh yeah, Henry helped a little.

Just kidding! He was fantastic. The best crew ever, after you.

Gilbert was sad that I replaced him, but he crewed for Cal and they came in second! He didn't seem so sad after that. He's turned out to be a decent sailor. I taught him everything he knows.

Of course, that means Cal and Gilbert beat Webby and Kevin. Probably because Kevin kept dragging his arm in the water, which slowed them down. Webby yelled at him the whole race.

"What?" Kevin yelled back. "I'm *hot*!"

It was a hot day for June. Tempers were short as a bald man's hair, as Dad likes to say.

Third place is not bad. That's what I told Webby.

He didn't take that well.

At the trophy ceremony, Mr. Peeler called up Kevin and Webby and gave them a little silver cup. Then he called Cal and Gilbert and presented them with a slightly bigger silver cup. Webby booed them. Mr. Peeler warned Webby that he would disqualify him for poor sportsmanship if he didn't watch out.

Then Mr. Peeler called up me and Henry to give us our big first-place trophy. I braced myself for booing, but Webby was silent.

For about three seconds.

Then, as Henry and I raised the trophy in victory, Webby yelled, "Kiss! Kiss!"

"Webster, I warned you," Mr. Peeler said.

Webby strutted in front of us chanting, "Henry likes Claire! Henry likes Claire!" He seemed to be trying to whip the crowd into a frenzy, but it didn't work. People were just staring at him. So Webby tried it the other way around: "Claire likes Henry! Claire likes Henry!"

"Webster, sit down!" Mr. Peeler shouted.

Gilbert, meanwhile, jumped to my defense.

"No!" he cried. "Claire doesn't like Henry! She likes me!"

I stink-eyed him.

"I hope," Gilbert added.

I double stink-eyed him.

"Someday?"

I knew he was trying to help. So this time it was only half a stink eye.

That took the wind out of Webby's sails, anyway. Mr. Peeler disqualified him for poor sportsmanship, just like he said he would. He took away Webby's third-place cup.

Kevin protested, "What about me? I didn't do anything!"

Mr. Peeler said, "Sorry, Kevin. When the captain misbehaves, the crew pays the price."

"No fair!" Kevin shouted. Then he gave Webby a *quadruple* stink eye.

So Kevin was mad at Webby, and Webby was mad at me and Henry.

But Henry and I were very happy.

"I know you don't like me that way," I told him.

"And I know you don't like *me* that way," he said back. "We're only friends."

"There's nothing *only* about being friends! What could be better than being friends?"

"Being best friends."

"You're right. Being best friends is better." Then I thought for a second and said, "But you know what's even better than that?"

"What?" Henry asked.

"Best friends and *co-champions*!" I proclaimed.

Henry grinned. "That *is* unbeatable!"

And that's exactly what we were.

Happily,
Claire

54

Fifth Grade Is Finally Over

Dear Bess,

Today was the last day of school. Next year I'll go off-island to Choptank Middle School, where there are plenty of girls.

The end of the school year was a lot better than the beginning. No Dodgeball Massacre, for one thing. Henry and I are friends just like we used to be—better, even. Webby has stopped picking on me, mostly, and the other boys don't obey him like they used to. Three of them asked if they could crew for me in the regatta next fall! But I'll stick with Henry.

We have our graduation ceremony tomorrow, but Mr. Harper held a private mini-ceremony today, just for our class.

He made a medal for each fifth grader—cardboard covered in gold foil, hung with a ribbon—to commemorate something special we had done during the year. He called us up one by one in alphabetical order to receive our medals.

"Kevin Ames."

Kevin walked to the front of the room.

Mr. Harper said, "Kevin, I give you this medal in recognition of your Great Knowledge of Dinosaur History."

He hung the medal around Kevin's neck. We clapped and cheered, and Kevin took a bow and sat down. He seemed really happy about his medal. It's true—he knows more than anybody about the dinosaurs.

Here are some of the other awards Mr. Harper gave out:

Henry Long: Excellence in Drama for His Outstanding Portrayal of Ebenezer Scrooge.

Gilbert Mellencamp: The School Spirit Medal for Cheerfulness and Kindness.

Zachary Mendoza: Excellence in Notebook Organization and Class Gerbil Caretaking.

Webster Peterson: Lunchroom Manners, Most Improved, earned mostly by not throwing banana peels at people more than once a month.

Calvin Pitovsky: Grossest Social Studies Presentation.

Zachary Roth: Most Explosive Papier-Mâché Volcano.

Claire Warren: Exemplary Courage and Resilience in the Face of Unusual and Extraordinarily Difficult Conditions.

Which means being the only girl in school.

The boys clapped extra hard for me. They whistled and cheered. Maybe they were cheering harder for me because I come last in the alphabet and my medal meant the school year was finally over. Maybe they cheered because I'm part of island history. Maybe it's because I found Smuggler Joe's treasure map or won the regatta again. I don't know.

I choose to think it's because they like me.

I stayed late after school so I could make my last drawings on our clubhouse wall. I'm going to miss having an entire school bathroom to myself. And I'll miss drawing the story of my life on the wall.

I drew events from the whole school year on that wall. A lot happened in the fifth grade.

There was my feud with Webby, and my sadness about Henry. There were soccer games and the square dance and the school play, and sailing, and rides with Starshine and Bruno. There was bowling with Gabe and the Killer Deer attack and my birthday party. There was the day we found Smuggler Joe's treasure map.

For my final picture, I drew this scene—me with my medal of courage, Mr. Harper and the boys cheering.

The cave drawings are now finished. It's a record of my year as the only girl at Foyes Island Elementary School.

I took a picture of it because I know it will be painted over by next fall.

But that's okay. On to the next adventure.

Your friend forever,
Claire

Lavender and Scarlet are nothing alike. Scarlet is tall, pretty, and popular. Lavender is . . . well, none of these things. There's only one thing they know they have in common: the same birthday. They've never shared parties or swapped presents. But this year, because of two wishes that turn all too true, they will swap something much bigger than presents . . . Lavender and Scarlet are going to swap lives.

One girl. One boy. Two dogs in puppy love. This means trouble . . .

pugs
and
kisses

j.j. howard
Author of *Sit, Stay, Love*

SCHOLASTIC

Although Ana doesn't have a dog of her own, she does get to walk her neighbor's adorable pug, Osito. One day, Osito befriends another dog at the park, who just happens to belong to a cute boy named Calvin. Ana implies Osito is hers, which seems like no big deal—until Calvin shows up at her school! Suddenly, Ana finds her fibs multiplying. Will she fess up before her white lies catch up to her?

Sometimes friends, boys, and ballet can cause quite a meltdown . . .

sundae
my prince
will come

suzanne nelson
author of donut go
breaking my heart

wish

SCHOLASTIC

Malie's mom manages an ice cream parlor, but Malie's real love is ballet. When cute new boy Alonzo arrives from Italy, *his* true love is ice cream—gelato, to be exact. Alonzo offers Malie a deal: If she lets him help out at the parlor, she can take dance lessons from his mom, a famed ballerina. But as Malie pirouettes between the parlor and the ballet studio, things start to spin out of control. Can she find her happily ever after?

Read the latest  books!